LAST WORDS

"Listen . . . important," Dundee said.

He glared at Frank, his eyes blazing as he tried to force the words out before his body betrayed him. "Find them . . . Fort . . ."

The effort was too much. Gerry Dundee's eyes rolled up, and the tautness went out of his muscles. He sagged into the grass.

Frank and Joe stared at each other.

He'd left them a world of trouble, a desperate need to get help—and half a clue.

Books in THE HARDY BOYS CASEFILES™ Series

Available from ARCHWAY Paperbacks

THE HARDY BOYS CASEFILES NO. 28

COUNTDOWN TO TERROR

FRANKLIN W. DIXON

AN ARCHWAY PAPERBACK
Published by POCKET BOOKS
New York   London   Toronto   Sydney   Tokyo   Singapore

AN ARCHWAY PAPERBACK *Original*

An Archway Paperback published by
POCKET BOOKS, a division of Simon & Schuster Inc.
1230 Avenue of the Americas, New York, NY 10020

ISBN: 0-671-74662-6

First Archway Paperback printing June 1989

10 9 8 7 6 5 4 3

COUNTDOWN
TO TERROR

Chapter

1

"I TELL YOU, Frank, we're being suckered." Joe Hardy scowled at his older brother, slightly raising his voice over the drone of the jet engines. "I think Dad's sending us on a wild-goose chase to get us out of the way. He hasn't trusted us since his last case."

Detective cases were something both the Hardys and their father knew a lot about. Fenton Hardy was an internationally known private investigator, and his sons had often tangled with criminals. But their last case, *Nowhere to Run,* had pitted father against sons. Fenton had had the job of capturing a friend of Frank's and Joe's, while the younger Hardys had tried to clear him. It put a serious strain on the family for a while—Joe was still feeling it.

Frank Hardy's dark eyes went from the news magazine he was reading to his brother's troubled face. "Chill out, Joe. Dad just asked us to do him a favor—fly up to Halifax, Nova Scotia, and pick up some depositions. I don't think he's sending us into exile."

"No, just all the way to Canada," Joe said sarcastically.

He got a shrug from Frank in reply. "Okay, this insurance scam may not be the biggest case ever to come our way. But we take what we can get." Frank tapped the magazine in his hand. "Maybe you'd rather be tackling this terrorist thing—twenty people killed in Europe and the Middle East, and no one knows who's doing it, much less why."

"Crazies don't need a reason," Joe said, his blue eyes suddenly icy. He'd lost a girlfriend, Iola Morton, in a terrorist bomb blast that had been meant for him. "Anyway, we'd be doing the world a favor if we went after scum like that. Who really cares about a bunch of penny-ante crooks fooling around with shipping cargoes to rook insurance companies?"

Frank grinned. "Well, the insurance companies do. And so does Dad, since he was hired to find these guys. And it's not so penny-ante. The accounts may be small, but these guys are operating up and down the whole Atlantic seaboard.''

The pitch of the ever-present hum of the engines changed, and the plane banked. ''We must be coming in for a landing,'' Joe said, looking out the window at a perfect late-summer day. ''Maybe a crash landing. I don't see anything out there but trees.''

Frank leaned across his brother to glance out the window. Thick pine forests, broken only here and there by lakes, rushed by under them. ''If you'd bothered to do a little homework instead of grousing about this trip, you'd know the airport is about six miles outside the city.''

''The control tower is probably made of logs,'' Joe muttered, still staring out the window.

But as the plane went into its landing glide, it approached an airport as modern as most. ''Looks like they use radar instead of smoke signals,'' Frank quipped to his brother.

The plane bounced once on the tarmac, then rolled to a stop beside the terminal. As soon as the moving walkway had been attached to the plane, the Hardys were ready to go. Both had carry-on bags—they hated waiting for luggage to be unloaded. Frank had a special padded flight bag for his lap-top computer. It hung from his shoulder as they walked off the plane.

''Let's grab a cab and get into town,'' Joe

said. "The sooner we finish this job, the happier I'll be."

Frank grinned at him. "You mean you don't want to hang around and enjoy all the tourist sights?"

Joe whipped around in the middle of the terminal, pulling something out of his pocket. "Well, if I'm here to play tourist, I brought the perfect prop."

With a flick, he opened a folding instant camera and hit the shutter switch. The built-in flash went off, and a moment later Joe handed Frank a picture of himself scowling against the glare of the flash.

"Perfect!" Now Joe was grinning.

Frank gave him a sour look. "I think you could use a little practice with this thing. Who are all these people behind me?"

"Local color," Joe loftily informed him.

They headed outside to the rank of taxicabs. Frank happened to glance back and saw one of the "local-color" people rushing over to a phone booth. He was a tall, dark guy with a bushy mustache and a white turban. "I hope he's not calling his lawyer about being blinded by a camera flash," he muttered. Then he slid in next to his brother in the cab.

It was an old luxury car, a "gas guzzler" with a surprisingly plush interior. Frank had noticed that the taxi sign on the roof was held on by tension cords. He suspected the car also served as the driver's personal transportation.

"The Harbour Hotel, please," Joe told the driver, and the car pulled smoothly away from the curb.

As soon as they were on the road, Joe rolled down the window, breathing deeply to take in the piney smell of the trees around them. "It's not exactly the way I expected to be introduced to a city," he said.

"Oh, Halifax is big," the driver said. "But it's green too." Passing through rolling hills heavily studded with stands of trees, the Hardys agreed that it did look pretty terrific.

"Not much traffic this afternoon," the driver continued. "You boys must have been the first off the plane."

"That's the best part of carrying your own bags," Joe said, staring out at the nearly empty road. "You mean you get traffic jams out here?"

"We get a lot of people on these roads," the driver said. "It's the worst on the bridges into town." He smiled. "Halifax has about everything you'd expect from a modern city, including traffic jams and crowds."

"And crazy drivers," Frank put in, looking out the front windshield. A red sports car had appeared at the top of the hill ahead, barreling down the gentle slope at full speed.

5

Joe laughed. "Maybe he's afraid he's going to miss his plane," he suggested.

The driver shook his head. "I don't think any flights are leaving right now," he said. "My bet is that he was supposed to pick someone up."

Soon after the red sports car flashed past them, they heard the shriek of its brakes. Frank looked out the rear window and saw the car go into a wild, fishtailing U-turn. Now it was moving up behind them.

Frank's eyes narrowed. There was something weird about this.

Joe's danger antennae were working just as well. "Driver, speed up a little," he said. "This guy is getting a little too close to our tail."

"You said it," the driver agreed. He hit the gas, and the big old car lengthened the distance between them.

But the red car sped up even more, as if it were trying to catch them.

"First he's in a hurry to go one way, then the other," the driver said. "I'm going to pull over and let this maniac pass."

"That's not—" Frank began.

"Don't!" Joe said.

But as they were speaking, the driver was tapping his brakes and pulling off to the side of the road.

Now the red car was slowing, too. As it came

up broadside, Frank watched as the passenger window steadily slid down. "Somehow, I don't think this guy needs directions," he said. "Let's get moving."

The driver turned back to stare at Frank blankly.

"Forget it," Joe yelled. *"Duck!"*

A hand had appeared in the sports car's window. It held a gleaming 9 mm automatic.

And it was pointed straight at them.

Chapter

2

THE HARDYS AND their driver hit the floor as the gunman cut loose with five wild shots. The windshield shattered, as well as both windows on the driver's side.

Although they couldn't see the red sports car from their positions on the floor, they heard the engine rev, the tires spin out.

"They're pulling out in front of us," Joe said. "We've got to get out of here."

He reached for the door handle, but missed as the taxi suddenly jerked forward. The engine roared as it picked up speed and passed the sports car.

Frank peered between the front seats to see the driver still on the floor, one hand holding the bottom of the steering wheel, the other on the gas pedal.

"How do you expect to steer—by touch?" Frank asked.

"Son," the driver said, "in the wintertime, when white-outs hit the road, that's just how we do drive. It beats getting shot at."

He jockeyed the wheel and chanced a darting glance into the rearview mirror. As his head rose above the seat, bullets smashed what was left of the rear window.

The driver tromped on the gas pedal, and the cab shot forward.

Frank and Joe looked back through the glass shards to see the red sports car starting up.

Both cars raced along the empty road in a weird dance. The agile red sports car darted back and forth behind the huge blue cab, trying to catch up. But the Hardys' driver sent his cab weaving across the road to block the attackers.

The gunman was leaning out the window, trying for a clear shot, when the cab slowed suddenly. The red car bounced off its rear fender. The impact nearly threw the gunman out of the car.

He shouted angrily, pumping bullets into the cab's trunk.

The driving battle continued, speed versus size. But finally the little car managed to maneuver around the larger one again. It swung wide, so that the gunman was even with the rear seats of the cab.

He grinned, raising his automatic.

Joe stared across the three-foot distance and into the eyes of his would-be murderer. He ducked and looked desperately around the backseat of the car, looking for something, *anything* to use in his defense.

Frank's computer lay on the seat beside him. Joe snatched up the flight bag by the shoulder strap and swung it out the shattered window.

It caught the gunman in the arm, deflecting his aim up. Still holding on to the bag, Joe leaned out of the car and swung his shoulder. This time the computer hit the gunman with stunning force, knocking him back against the sports car's driver.

The car veered closer to the cab as Joe leaned out farther, swinging the bag over his head. Frank reached out to his brother, trying to steady him.

Then Joe released the whirling bag, sending it straight into the oncoming car's windshield. It smashed against the glass, shattering it into a spider's web of cracks.

The driver flinched, losing control of the car, which careened wildly across the road into a stand of white birches.

Frank pulled his eyes away from the scene.

"Nice aim. But did you have to use my computer?"

The wrecked car quickly receded behind them. Joe leaned forward to tap their driver on the shoulder. "Hey, aren't we going to stop?"

"Not as long as those guys have guns," the driver told him. "We'll call the cops at the first gas station we come to."

The Hardys shrugged. They weren't eager to face the gunman again either. "Maybe we should call Dad's contact on the Halifax force," Joe said.

Frank nodded. "It'd be easier than trying to explain this to a desk sergeant."

They were pulling up at a gas station then. "We'll call the police," Frank said.

"And you'd better call a cab," the driver said. "This one is a little too open to the wind."

Frank got the number for the Halifax police, dialed, and asked for Sergeant Gerald Dundee. The desk officer transferred his call.

"Dundee," a voice snapped on the other end of the line.

"Sergeant Dundee, this is Frank Hardy—my brother and I are supposed to meet you this afternoon. But something very strange has happened on the way in from the airport." He gave the story of the attack.

Frank ended the story, "Either they wanted

11

us, or they wanted the car we were in. Who knew we were coming?"

"Myself and the insurance people," Dundee replied. "It was hardly top secret. But why would a bunch of insurance cheats attack you?" Dundee had grown much less annoyed as he listened to Frank's story. "Tell the driver to stay at the gas station until I get there. You go on to your hotel—the Harbour, isn't it? I'll come and question you after I'm finished out there."

Even as Frank was hanging up, a new taxi arrived. The Hardys transferred their bags, then gave their first driver Dundee's message and paid him. They felt it was the least they could do.

The rest of the ride into the city of Halifax was quiet. They came to a wide expanse of water—Halifax Harbor—which they had to cross to enter the city. "This is the old bridge," the driver said as he started across a two-lane span. "Up north is the newer bridge."

The Hardys looked out at the bustling seaport. The cranes were moving boxcar-size crates into the holds of waiting container ships. Other ships were moored at the docks—including a navy corvette.

When they were across the bridge and driving through the city, they were impressed with the mix of state-of-the-art office towers with buildings from one or two centuries before. The driver pulled past what looked like two-hundred-year-old warehouses to stop in front of an ultramodern hotel complex. "The Harbour Hotel," he said. "Right next to the old and restored part of town."

"Very impressive," Frank said. He and Joe paid their fare, got their bags, registered, and settled into their hotel room to wait for Sergeant Dundee.

He arrived about an hour later, a big, craggy-faced man with ginger red hair turning to white. Heavy, grizzled eyebrows topped his piercing blue eyes. He was vigorous, but he was old. Frank realized Dundee must be near retirement age. That was why he'd been given the job of dealing with insurance companies and their investigators. Judging from the heavy frown lines cut into the man's face, he didn't enjoy his job.

But Dundee's eyes sparkled with life as he filled the Hardys in on the investigation into the attack. "There's little enough to be said— the car was empty when we got to it. We're checking the plates, of course. And I found some blank import forms in the glove compartment."

He smiled. "We may have some sort of smuggling operation involved here."

"Isn't that a little out of your line?" Joe

asked. "I thought you were the local insurance liaison—"

Dundee cut him off bitterly. "I've spent years on the force—most of them on the waterfront. And my contacts down there can track these guys down faster than anyone else."

Joe shrugged, aware he had touched a nerve.

"Is there anything we can do?" Frank asked.

Dundee shook his head. "I'll take care of this investigation. If you remember anything more though, contact me."

Sergeant Dundee rose from the couch in the hotel room and headed for the door. "If you show up at my office tomorrow morning, I'll have those depositions ready." He opened the door and turned back to them. "You should be able to leave town by tomorrow afternoon."

He closed the door so sharply behind him that it was almost a slam. Frank turned to his brother. "Do you get the feeling he wants us out of his way?"

"I think he's too busy trying to prove that he's still a cop to worry about us." He stretched and patted his stomach. "Right now, I'm more worried about what's for dinner."

They went exploring the city's waterfront restoration project and found intriguing small shops and lots of restaurants. Joe stopped in front of one place that had a sign with a man in uniform scoffing up a huge meal. "The Hungry Guardsman," he said, reading the sign. "Home of the three-dollar steak. Sounds good to me."

"There are lots of people inside," Frank said, looking through the window.

"And lots of cute girls," Joe added, pressing close to the window.

They went inside, and a waitress in a striped jersey showed them to a table. "Give us a couple of Cokes," Joe said, "and two of those three-dollar steaks."

"Oh," said the girl, "I'll send the food waitress right over."

"Food waitress?" Joe gave her a puzzled look.

"I only serve from the bar," the girl said.

Joe shrugged. "Well, do what you have to do. We're here to eat." He grinned. "But I don't think another waitress could be as cute as you."

He was wrong. When the other girl arrived, she put her coworker in the shade. Mischievous blue eyes twinkled above a cute snub nose with just a sprinkling of freckles. She gave them a quick grin. "Hi, I'm Shauna MacLaren. I'm your server tonight." she said. "I hear you'd like some food." She was a tall girl, just an inch or two shorter than Joe's six feet. On her model-perfect frame the restaurant's informal uniform of striped jersey and jeans looked like a fashion statement. Her shoulder-length hair was midnight black.

"I—wow!" Joe sat back and stared.

"What my talkative friend here wanted to say was that we'd like a couple of those three-dollar steaks," Frank told Shauna.

She brought them the steaks in moments, and the boys dug in.

"Frank"—Joe looked up, his mouth half full of steak and fries—"remember how I told you never to let me fall for a waitress again?"

The second great love of Joe's life had been a Bayport waitress, Annie Shea, who'd nearly gotten him killed in the *Witness to Murder* case.

Frank nodded. "I remember."

"Well, I want you to forget it." Joe's eyes followed Shauna as she walked among the tables.

"I should have guessed," Frank groused. "But I warn you, she's getting you into trouble already."

"What are you talking about?" Joe demanded.

"You've been so busy keeping an eye on her, you didn't notice those guys at the table behind us. They came in right after us, and they've been watching us ever since."

Joe turned, pretending to watch Shauna

while actually scanning the room. "You think we've got a tail?"

"Well, there's one way to find out." Frank abruptly rose from his seat, tossing a ten on the table. Joe gave one sad glance to what was left of his steak and stood up, too. The three guys who'd been eating behind them abandoned their meals. It was the proof the Hardys needed.

"They're between us and the door," Joe said.

"I know—we'll take another exit." Frank had already noticed another door that opened onto a small sidewalk dining area. Leading Joe, he walked through the diner, over the knee-high fence that separated the tables from the traffic, and down the street.

The tails took the same route, blank faced.

"They've got to know we're on to them," Joe whispered. "What will they do now?"

His answer came as four more rugged-looking types joined the three guys.

"I don't like this," Frank said. "Come on!"

He darted into traffic and across the street, then turned right. They were on a very busy boulevard that led up a steep hill to an open park. The seven trackers began closing in.

Joe glanced over at his brother. "If we're going to run, it's easier downhill," he said.

Frank nodded. "On the count of three, we cross back, and run down. One—two—"

He waited until a bus blocked the pursuers from crossing the road, then called, "Three!"

Frank and Joe dashed in front of the bus, then down the hill.

The tails were caught flat-footed and couldn't pursue until after Frank and Joe had a decent lead.

Joe glanced back, grinning at the guys behind them. "What do we do now?" he asked.

"We stop," Frank said.

Joe stared at his brother. "Why?"

"We just ran out of running room," Frank answered.

Their escape route dead-ended—right into Halifax Harbor.

Chapter

3

THE HARDYS HAD only two ways out of this disaster—to the right or to the left, along the water.

To the left Joe saw quays and tourist joints. Far in the distance rose the Harbour Hotel, a possible haven that might as well be on Mars.

"This way!" Frank was looking right—to a sign that read Ferry Passengers.

The ferry terminal was just beyond that, and beyond that the ferry. Late commuters were boarding, and it was obvious the ship was about to leave.

Joe didn't need to be told twice. Both Hardys darted to the right. As they entered the terminal building, they were confronted by a line of turnstiles. But Joe saw a sign by the snack bar that said Tokens. Still on the run, he slapped down the necessary fares and got two tokens.

He and Frank were through the turnstiles and boarding just as the pursuing posse stormed into the terminal. The loading gates came up, and the ferry pulled away. Joe waved goodbye to the seven furious faces.

"Looks like they missed the boat," he said.

Frank nodded. "I just wonder where we're going." He dug into his jacket pocket and came out with a guidebook. Paging through, he smiled. "We're going to a town called Dartmouth, just across the harbor. And I know exactly where we're heading once we get there."

Joe stared at him. "Where?"

"To a phone—we've got to call Sergeant Dundee."

Until then, they enjoyed the view of Halifax Harbor—from the middle of the water.

When the ferry pulled into Dartmouth Terminal, Frank and Joe joined the stream of commuters onto dry land again. There was a pay phone in the terminal building, and Frank dialed Dundee's number.

On the third ring the phone was picked up. "Dundee's line," a clipped voice on the other end answered from what was obviously a squad room.

Frank identified himself and asked for Sergeant Dundee. He was told the policeman wasn't in at the moment, but that he'd return Frank's call if he'd leave a number. "If you mean right away, he can get us at 555-8912," Frank said, reading the number on the phone. "It's a pay phone."

"We'll get him," the voice promised.

The police were as good as their word. Almost as soon as Frank hung up, the phone rang. Gerry Dundee was on the other end.

"Sergeant Dundee, Frank Hardy here," Frank said. "I've got a follow-up report for you." He went on to explain how he and Joe had been followed and how they'd escaped.

"So now you're in the ferry terminal on the Dartmouth side, eh?" Dundee said. "Cross the rail line there, cross Windmill Road, then head up Portland Street. The first place on the right-hand side is a cops' hangout. Wait for me there and you shouldn't have any trouble. I'll be along in fifteen to twenty minutes."

Frank hung up the phone, turned to Joe, and said, "We get to take a little walk."

They followed Dundee's directions, found the place, and spent the next few minutes peering out the window at the street one floor below. It wasn't long before an unmarked car pulled up outside the place. Gerry Dundee stepped out.

He was in a very good mood when he met the Hardys. "So you had to cut your dinner short over there across the water," he said. "Let's make up for it over here—my treat."

Dundee ushered them over to a table, and moments later they were sitting in front of thick, steaming steaks. "Always a favorite of mine," he said, tucking in with the gusto of a man twenty years younger.

He smiled at Joe's slightly surprised look. "The smart mouths in the department wonder how I can tackle these, too," he said. "In their books, old crocks like myself don't have the teeth—or the brains—for real meat or real cases."

Spearing another hunk of medium-rare beef, he popped it into his mouth and began chewing. Then he swallowed and smiled. "They think that once you get to a certain age, you can't take it anymore."

He tapped the side of his head. "But this old brain has more experience and data locked away than all their precious computers. I've found out some stuff—"

Frank asked suddenly, not meaning to interrupt but impatient for news, "Anything said about our case?"

Dundee drew himself up, his face going stiff. "What are you talking about?"

"I mean what was the reaction from your buddies downtown. You'd think they'd show some interest when somebody involved in an attack like the one we went through gave you a call. But the guy I talked to acted as if he'd never heard of me."

Dundee didn't reply. He just stared stonily at Frank.

Frank leveled his gaze and returned the stare.

"Are you investigating this case on your own?"

Nothing. No reply.

"If I'd wanted a one-man show on this case I'd have turned to my brother Joe and let him carry the ball. But we did the right thing; we contacted the police."

Frank leaned across the table. "So, you're holding on to the report on our attack—hiding the facts in your head, with all that other great data. Well, I don't like it. I don't like being staked out like a sacrificial lamb while you try to breathe some life into your career."

"Hey, Frank," Joe began, looking from his brother to Dundee as they continued to glare at each other, "I'd like to hear what he has to say."

23

He turned to Dundee, but the older cop's face was still a frozen mask.

Gerald Dundee reached into his pocket, threw enough money down on the table to cover the tab, and rose abruptly from his seat. "I don't have to justify myself to anyone, especially to a kid like you," he said. "I've put in enough time on the job to know what I'm doing."

He stepped away from the table and headed for the stairs that led down to the street. "If you want a lift back to the Harbour Hotel, I'll give it to you. But we won't discuss the case."

Joe wanted to discuss it, but judging from the looks on his brother's and Dundee's faces, he knew his chance for learning anything that night was blown.

Joe looked unhappily at his half-eaten meal for the second time that night. At least the lift would get them back to their hotel quickly. Maybe the Harbour Hotel had steak on its room-service menu.

"Uh, thanks, Sergeant," Joe said. "*I'd* appreciate the lift." He glanced over at Frank, giving him a look that said, "Cool it—one of us should stay friendly with this guy."

They walked down the stairs to the restaurant exit, Joe walking with Dundee, Frank trailing behind. It felt funny for Joe to be playing

the nice guy—especially when they were playing the game with a cop.

Dundee led the way to the unmarked car,
opening the doors. "I'm afraid one of you will
have to ride in the back."

Frank silently took the rear seat, usually
reserved for suspects and prisoners. Joe took
the shotgun seat, right in front of the car's
police radio.

Gerry Dundee stepped around the car to get
behind the steering wheel. He started the engine and pulled the car away from the sidewalk.

"Hand me that mike, Joe," he said as they
drove down the street. "I should call in and let
the dispatcher know I'm back in the car."

Joe handed over the microphone, and Dundee hit the button on the side. "Car ninety-
seven to base—I'm heading back to town."

There was a brief burst of static, then a voice
came back, "What's the matter, Gerry? The
steak over there too tough for you nowadays?"

That got a flash of a grin from Dundee.
Obviously he and the dispatcher were old
friends. "Helen, *life* is tough—not the steaks."

While Dundee and the dispatcher bantered,
Frank leaned over from the back seat, listening
intently.

"What's that noise?" he asked suddenly.

Dundee glanced over his shoulder, his face
hardening again. "What noise?"

They all could hear it now, over the open line—brief, tiny blips of interference, coming regularly.

Frank frowned as he listened, his eyes searching the interior of the car. "Those blips are some kind of FM broadcast—and since they're not getting any softer or louder, I guess whatever's causing them is in this car."

"So?" Dundee wanted to know.

"So," Frank answered, "the only thing I can think of that would make that noise is a radio-controlled bomb."

His face was grim as he turned to the others. "And I think we're riding right on top of it."

Chapter

4

GERRY DUNDEE LICKED his lips nervously.

"Son," he said, "you picked a great time to tell me that."

Frank and Joe looked up from the search they'd been making of the car to stare at what was happening around them.

Dundee had just turned onto a busy road. They were jammed in the middle of traffic now.

"We can't bail out here," Joe said. "Where does this road go?"

"Straight to the bridge," Dundee said, his voice tight. "If we blow up anywhere along here, we'll take dozens of people with us."

Frank's eyes darted right and left. "Can't

we turn off and head for someplace less congested?"

Dundee shrugged. "We can try to turn left up here—if we don't get killed by the bridge traffic."

He was going to try for the left-hand lane, but a car screeched up beside theirs just then, cutting them off. The bridge toll stations were ahead of them now. They were stuck on the bridge, like it or not.

Frank turned to the left and stared at the passenger in the car that cut them off. He looked familiar. Frank placed him almost immediately. He was the guy with the mustache and turban he'd seen hurrying for a phone in the airport. It was definitely the same guy.

Now Mr. Mustache held up a small box with a whip-aerial and a button on it. The message was clear. This was the detonator for the bomb they had on board.

"I don't think they're going to blow us up as long as we're good boys," Frank said. "That guy hasn't made a move to touch the button."

"That wouldn't be smart, with us right beside him," Joe pointed out. "I don't think it would do the bridge much good, either."

"I think they're just going to use it as a threat to get us to park someplace nice and quiet where they can question us, but about what I don't know."

Frank sounded calm, but his brain was churning furiously, trying to come up with a way out of this death trap. Right then, he reasoned, they did have one slim advantage. The enemy, whoever they were, didn't want them dead—at least not yet.

"If we let them pace us all the way, we'll never have a chance of escaping," he said. "Sergeant, can you get ahead of them?"

"On a jam-packed bridge?" Dundee asked. But he nodded his head, realizing they might be able to use the distance. "I'll do my best."

A tiny opening developed in the left-hand lane, ahead of their pursuers. Gerry Dundee shouldered his car into it. Then he darted back into another small open spot in the lane next to it, earning a blast on the horn from the driver he had cut off.

They'd gained a bare car length, but the pursuit car was having a hard time catching up. Drivers who've been cut off once aren't willing to let it happen again soon.

Dundee continued to weave through the heavy traffic. It was slow going, pulling a half a car length here, a half a car length there. But as the far end of the bridge came up, they were still within plain sight of their pursuers.

The pursuit car pulled over to the right-hand lane to be in the same one as Dundee. The older policeman grinned.

"Good. They think I'm going to make the right off the bridge and take the underpass to Barrington Street. Well, they're in for a surprise."

He accelerated past the turnoff and whipped into the left lane. Then he made a wild left turn, nearly getting clipped by a horrified van driver. "Get ready to jump, boys," Dundee said as he jockeyed the wheel. "This street dead-ends into a sort of park that should be deserted now."

Frank and Joe saw the greenery up ahead as Dundee swerved to the right side of the road. "Get while the getting's good!" he yelled, jamming on the brakes.

The Hardys jumped. Dundee brought the car around in a screeching U-turn, pretending that he'd just discovered the road didn't go through.

Then the pursuit car rolled up to block the open end of the street.

Gerry Dundee was already halfway out of the car, with one foot on the pavement.

Mr. Mustache must have hit the button, because two seconds later the unmarked car blew up.

Frank and Joe were staggered by the blast. It tore the hood off the engine and shattered the windshield. It also tossed Gerry Dundee like a rag doll in a tornado.

He flew across the street, arms flailing, and

landed hard on the grassy ground near the Hardys.

Joe stared at the man lying unmoving near his feet. Frank was looking at the guys in the pursuit car. Apparently they decided they'd called too much attention to themselves. With a screech of rubber, they peeled out and away from there.

Frank turned to his brother, who was kneeling beside Dundee. "Don't try to move him," he said, putting a hand on Joe's arm to stop him. "He may have internal injuries—and we don't want to make a bad situation worse."

Dundee had landed half on his side, half on his stomach, his arm twisted under him. His face lay in the dirt. Slowly, painfully, he turned his head around. Spotting Frank, he sucked in a shallow breath.

At first Frank thought Dundee was just wheezing. Then he realized Dundee was trying to tell him something. "Easy, easy," he said, dropping down to his knees beside the injured man. "Don't move around."

Gerry Dundee ignored him, trying to twist around, trying to talk. Half the man's face was bruised and beginning to swell. He winced as he coughed—it sounded more like a death rattle. Frank had horrible visions of broken ribs and vulnerable lungs as Dundee kept mouthing words at him. He had no breath to sustain an actual sound.

To try to stop him, Frank brought his ear close to Dundee's mouth. Even then he could barely understand what the old cop was gasping out.

"Listen . . . important," Dundee said. "Found out . . . where . . . are." He glared at Frank, his eyes blazing for a moment as he tried to force the words out before his body betrayed him. "Find them . . . Fort . . ."

The effort was too much. Gerry Dundee's eyes rolled up, and the tautness went out of his muscles. He sagged down into the grass.

Frank and Joe stared at each other. He'd left them a world of trouble, a desperate need to get help—and half a clue.

Chapter

5

THE HARDYS STOOD surrounded by a sea of blue uniforms in the waiting room of the Camp Hill Hospital. They all wanted word of Gerry Dundee. Instead of a white-coated surgeon, however, a guy in a suit separated himself from the figures in police blue to talk to the boys. He didn't need to present his ID and badge. Everything about him said plainclothes cop.

"What can we do for you, Detective Otley?" Frank asked, glancing at the man's identification. He and Joe knew only too well what was coming.

"It's a shame about poor Gerry," Otley told them. "My father worked with him once. He was a legend on the waterfront—nothing went on there that he didn't know about." The police officer shook his head again. "Those days are long past now."

Otley looked at them with about four thousand questions in his eyes. "Now, about this report you gave the uniformed officers," he went on. "You said you reported being attacked on the road from the airport. I've checked, and we have no record of any such report."

Frank shrugged. "I was asking Sergeant Dundee about that when we realized there was a bomb in his car."

The detective gave them a sharp glance. "That's another part of your story I'd like to hear more about. I'm sure you know that Gerry Dundee is semiretired, working only as our insurance liaison. He wasn't even investigating any large cases. So why would anyone plant a bomb in his car?"

"Maybe he wasn't investigating anything *officially*," Joe said, "but something must have been up. "Take a look at the car—that damage didn't happen because he'd forgotten to change his oil filter."

They spent another hour talking with Otley, then the news came from surgery. "Sergeant Dundee is in very critical condition," the doctor said. "We've moved him to the intensive care unit."

"He's not conscious yet?" Otley asked.

The doctor shook his head. "At this point, it's touch and go whether he'll ever regain consciousness."

Otley and the Hardys decided there was nothing they could do and began to leave. Frank looked at the detective. "How about what Dundee said after the explosion?" he asked. "I could hardly make out the words, but it was something about finding someone at a fort."

Detective Otley bit back a laugh. "Halifax was the main British base in eastern Canada. This area is *crawling* with forts."

Frank and Joe were silent as Otley gave them a lift. They'd given him the name of a different hotel—the Cavalier—and all the way there, they looked back for tails.

After registering, Frank said, "Well, if they're not going to check out the forts, I guess we will."

The next morning found the boys buying new clothes—they had left their luggage at the first hotel. Frank spent time the night before with a map and guide to Halifax, choosing sites. "We'll work our way back," he said. "Our first stop is Fort Needham Park."

They found the park easily enough, perched on top of a high hill. But they didn't find a fort—just a brass plaque, indicating that a fort had once stood there.

Joe stared around. "Somehow, I don't think this is the fort Dundee meant. I'd have a hard time imagining the bad guys hanging out here," he said, gesturing to a playground.

Frank was looking at the strange monument that stood in the middle of the park, a thirty-foot-long cement wall with an arch and old-fashioned church bells hanging from it. He and Joe went over to check it out.

"It's a monument to the *Imo* disaster," he said, reading a plaque. "Back in World War I, a ship full of artillery shells collided with a ship, the *Imo*, in the harbor here." The park had a perfect view of the waterway out of the harbor.

"According to one of the guidebooks I read last night, a quarter of the city was destroyed. The whole area behind us was blown flat."

Joe looked back along the quiet streets lined with neat houses made of concrete block. "Yeah—those houses all look like they were built at the same time," he said. "That must have been quite a blast."

Frank nodded. "It was the biggest man-made explosion until the atomic bomb went off over Hiroshima." He shook his head. "They found pieces of wreckage twenty miles away."

"Well, that's interesting, but we are looking for a fort," Joe said. "Where do we go now?"

Frank told him and then led the way down Gottingen Street to central Halifax. It must once have been a bustling shopping area, but now many of the stores were boarded up, and others looked pretty seedy. Then they began climbing again, a different hill, steeper than the first. Joe read a sign that said The Citadel.

"This is the biggest of the old fortifications," Frank said. "I think we should check it out."

"But wouldn't he have said *citadel* instead of *fort?*" Joe asked.

The wound their way up a path that climbed the hill. Slowly the fortress came into view. The outside of the wall was a grassy hill, which protected the inside granite wall from cannon fire. Frank and Joe joined a stream of tourists entering through the only gate, a thin bridge across a ditch.

"Quite a place," Joe said, looking around the stone walls, which butted up to the hill.

"Complete with Hungry Guardsmen," Frank said, watching as a file of red-coated young soldiers in kilts came marching up. Another young soldier not in formation walked by just then and stopped beside them.

"You've been to the Hungry Guardsman?" he asked, smiling. "It's one of our favorite hangouts—out of uniform, that is." He glanced down at his finery. "When school's on we go there for lunch."

"School?" Joe asked.

"You didn't think we were full-time soldiers, did you?" the young corporal asked. "This is a summer job, to help pay for college." He grinned under his jaunty Scots highland bonnet. "We study the drillbooks from 1869 and our routines are completely authentic. Watch us put on our show." He pulled out an old-fashioned pocket watch. "And you should stay for the firing of the noon gun."

Another officer strolled over. "Corporal Bell, shouldn't you be at your post?"

Bell snapped to attention. "Yes, *sir!*" He trotted off to join the marching troops.

Lining up, the summer soldiers went through the drill of loading and firing their weapons like well-trained professionals. The crowd was firing away, too, clicking cameras like mad.

"That must take a lot of practice," Joe said, watching as the troopers reloaded and fired again. Even though they were firing blanks, the sharp crack! of the volleys was pretty deafening.

"There sure is a crowd," Frank said. "I don't think the guys we're looking for would hang around—"

He bit off his words suddenly as he recognized a face and turban at the edge of the crowd. It was the guy from the airport and the pursuit car, Mr. Mustache.

Apparently, he realized he'd been spotted. As the Hardys tried to push their way to him, he was already moving across the drill grounds, heading for the ramp up to the earthen parapets of the fort. Once on top he ducked to the left, disappearing behind the roof of the powder magazine, the room where explosives were stored.

Frank and Joe ran after him, but when they reached the top of the ramp, they didn't see the white turban.

"He can't have gone far," Joe said. "But those crowds are blocking the way around to the other walls."

Frank nodded. "Looks like the noon gun is about to be set off."

More student-soldiers had appeared, these in dark blue uniforms with pillbox caps. They were wheeling back a cannon at the far edge of the wall, preparing it to be fired.

"I don't see him in the crowd," Joe said. "So where is he?"

Frank was staring thoughtfully along the top ridge of the earthen fortification. Two holes broke the line of the wall. Apparently they were dugout rooms that burrowed down into the hillside.

Joe followed his brother's gaze. "Let's check 'em out."

The entrance to the first dugout was locked, but the door to the second one lay open. They went down a couple of steps, through a doorway, and into a cramped stone room like a cellar. There was a large sign warning troops not to smoke or carry lit matches into this ammunition room. Joe was just peering into a separate chamber beyond when the door slammed shut behind them.

Frank pounded once on the door before realizing that it opened inward. But when he pulled the latch, the door didn't open either. It had been jammed shut.

Still heaving at the door, Frank said, "Joe, look in that other room and see if there's anything we can use for a tool."

Joe was in and out of the room in a second, his face white.

"What's the matter, old gunpowder storage areas make you nervous?" Frank kidded.

But after he spoke, he realized he was seeing some sort of blinking red glow from the other room.

"The ammunition in there is not old," Joe said. "Not unless they had digital timers back in 1869."

Chapter

6

FRANK FORGOT ABOUT the door and rushed into the other chamber. It was a bare, chilly, whitewashed room, with empty old gunpowder barrels.

But sitting on one of the white-painted shelves was something a lot newer. At first, all Frank saw were the flashing red numbers on the timer, ticking down from the three-minute mark. Then he saw the wires leading into a small metal box. A little bit of grayish-yellow gunk that looked like clay oozed out one corner.

Frank knew it wasn't clay—it was plastic explosive.

He moved to the bomb. "This is my job,"

he said quickly to Joe. "You work on trying to get that door open."

Joe ran for the outer door, yelling back, "Can you disarm that thing?"

"Do my best," Frank said. "But there's not much time. Whoever set this wants us to go off with the noontime gun."

"That guy must have been hiding on the far side of this dugout, then sneaked back and pulled the door closed." Joe's voice was full of disgust as he tugged at the door. "He suckered us just fine."

Frank was busy trying to follow the wires from the timer to the plastique. Some of them didn't seem to have any purpose. He took a deep breath and wiped his sweaty palms on his pants. They had to be decoys or booby traps. Two minutes, thirty seconds left.

He quickly traced a red wire into a complicated loop, where three other wires, black, yellow, and blue, twined in. Were they spliced in or just wound around it? Frank took a deep breath. "A Fellawi loop," he muttered out loud, startling himself.

"A what?" Joe asked. He'd given up trying to pull the door open and was now on his back, attempting brute force. He was kicking at it. But the thick old panels resisted him, and the noise of preparing to fire the gun covered any other noises he made.

"Omar Fellawi is the dean of terrorist bomb makers," Frank said, gently probing at the rat's nest of wires. "If the stories about him are true, he taught himself, and doesn't follow any of the usual methods." It calmed Frank to talk—it made it seem that he had time to kill. But he only had two minutes to detonation.

"I didn't know there were rules for making bombs."

"Oh, there are, and they're very strict," Frank said. "I've seen some of the manuals, and there are rules you have to memorize. 'Blue before yellow can kill a fellow.' That's one of them. It means if you disconnect the blue wire before the yellow one, it could set the bomb off." Frank sucked air in through his teeth. A wire had come away in his hand—a blue one.

"And you're saying Fellawi doesn't care what colors he uses?" Joe had jumped to his feet again, scraping away the paint from the door hinges with his pocketknife. But it didn't seem likely that he'd loosen the hinges before time ran out.

"A lot of bomb squad people died before they figured out what he was doing," Frank said, glancing at the timer. One minute, thirty seconds. "Not only that, but he uses these big loops of wire with colors twined together. It's his signature."

"But I guess now that they know about his tricks, they know how to get around them." Joe bit back a curse as the largest blade on his pocketknife snapped when he tried to wedge it under the hinge to lift it off.

"Fellawi thought of that. He keeps changing the colors he uses." Frank stopped trying to separate the wires and called in to Joe, "Bring that knife in here, please, and use this key for attacking that hinge."

Joe traded his knife for Frank's key. But when he returned to the door, he changed tactics and probed the oversize keyhole to see if he could knock loose whatever was jamming it.

Frank delicately traced along each wire with one of the knife's smaller blades. The yellow wire went from the loop to circle around the box containing the explosive, tying it up like a Christmas present. There was no way into the box without cutting the wire. Frank looked at the timer. His vision was blurred with sweat running off his forehead. A finger cleared it. Less than a minute left. He'd have to chance it.

Heart thudding against his chest cavity and blood roaring in his ears, Frank scraped away the insulation on the yellow wire in two places. He wrapped in the piece of loose blue wire. That gave him a bypass circuit—maybe. He slipped the knife under the yellow wire, took what could be his last breath, and slowly raised the knife and snapped the wire.

He didn't even look at the timer as he slipped the box free and frantically dug his way through the plastique.

One deft probe with his fingers and an electrical lead came out of the gook. More careful digging, and a walnut-size metal ball was uncovered. "Booby trap," Frank said. "It's a mercury switch. Any attempt to move the box around would have set it—and the bomb—off."

Just then the noon gun went off far over their heads. Frank loved the quiet inside the bunker. No bomb exploded. It *was* disarmed. Frank smiled, slapped his brother on the back, and remembered to breathe.

"How does it feel to deface Parks Canada property?" Joe asked as they finally removed the hinges and the door.

Frank cocked an eyebrow at him.

Frank and Joe headed down the ramp, then across the drill field toward the exit. "I think an anonymous call to the cops should take care of what's left in there," he said. "And if our friends try to remove the evidence, all the better. Maybe they'll be caught in the act."

They took a different path away from the

Citadel, going down a flight of stairs cut into the hillside.

"How come we're leaving the bad guys' headquarters?" Joe wanted to know as he trailed Frank.

"That's not their headquarters," Frank said. "I started to say that when we saw our friend with the turban. There's too much staff and too many tourists around for any funny business. That bomb there just confirms it."

"I don't get it," Joe said.

"Would you set off a bomb in your base of operations? An explosion would be sure to focus too much attention."

Joe frowned. "Then how come that guy— *and* that bomb—were there?"

"We had to be followed. They brought something up to take care of us and led us right to it." Frank struck off on a downhill street, heading back to Halifax Harbor.

"You think this guy is still tailing us?" Joe asked, glancing over his shoulder.

"I hope so—and don't try to warn him off," Frank said. "Our next stop will give us a chance to isolate him."

They came down on the far side of the ferry terminal, out onto some docks where excursion boats were moored. Frank stepped up to a wooden shack to buy two tickets as a guy with sandy blond hair came screeching up on a bike.

"You guys are lucky that I held up our departure to go to the bank."

They pocketed their tickets, then followed the man to one of the excursion boats already filled with tourists. He led them across the deck, up a staircase, onto the top sundeck, then into the deckhouse. "Ready to cast off!" he called to his two crewmen.

Joe stared. "You're the captain?"

The guy grinned back. "Of the McNab's Island Ferry.

Joe turned to Frank. "So *that's* where we're going."

Frank smiled at Joe. "There're a couple of forts out there." Then he turned to the captain. "Can you hold off for a few more minutes?"

"Why?" the captain wanted to know.

Frank smiled. "I think you'll be getting one more customer."

Sure enough, the turbaned guy with the mustache came tearing down to the pier. The bad news was, there were about six other guys with him. Frank and Joe recognized most of them from their marathon to the ferry the day before.

"Well, you wanted to isolate him," Joe whispered to Frank.

"Looks like I've isolated us instead." Frank

asked the captain, "Mind if we stay up here? We'd like to see you work the harbor."

The captain grinned. "I'd like that. Most people are a little shy about coming up here."

Even the army of seven felt shy. They stayed down on the lower deck, glaring up at the Hardys.

Meanwhile the captain steered a course though Halifax Harbor to the island.

"You know, McNab's Island has a lot of history behind it," the captain said as they slipped into a wide cove with a single large pier. To the south, a neck of land jutted out, a lighthouse on its tip.

"That's Hangman's Beach," the captain said, nodding to the outthrust land. "They used to hang mutineers out there." He shook his head. "There're a lot of bodies—about ten thousand buried under that sand. The French sent an expedition here, and they based themselves on McNab's until storms and sickness nearly wiped them out."

"Where's the fort?" Joe asked.

"Which one?" the captain asked. "Fort Ives is at the north end, and Fort McNab is in the south." He grinned. "Fort McNab is the bigger draw."

Frank asked, "How far to McNab?"

"About a mile and a half from the pier," the captain said.

They were pulling up beside the pier now. A gravel road ran beside the beach, and Frank saw a pickup truck heading toward the pier.

Joe saw it, too. He turned to the captain. "Mind if we help tie up?"

The captain shrugged and reversed engines. Frank and Joe leapt from the sundeck to the pier, tossed the mooring ropes onto their pilings, and ran for the road.

They'd reached the beach before their pursuers had even gotten through the crowd gathered at the gangplank to the pier. Frank was already flagging the pickup down.

"Are you heading anywhere near Fort McNab?" he asked.

The driver leaned out the window. "I can take you partway," he said. "You in a hurry?"

Joe glanced at the thugs elbowing their way through people toward them—blood in their eyes.

"You *could* say that," he admitted.

Chapter

7

THE PICKUP PULLED away as Frank and Joe's pursuers came tearing down the pier.

When he saw the newcomers, the driver slowed. "They want to come, too?"

Frank talked fast. "Keep going—please! It's a scavenger hunt—the first team to reach the fort wins the point."

"Okay." The driver zipped off, leaving the mob behind. So far, none of the pursuers had pulled guns, although the Hardys had noticed suspicious bulges under several of the guys' jackets.

"Looks like they've been told to take us quietly," Joe said. "No witnesses."

"Maybe," Frank said. "But where we're

going, there don't seem to be many tourists."
He stared over the top of the cab as they
bounced along the deeply rutted gravel road.
Ragged trees leaned over them, and the farther
they traveled, the more deserted the island
became.

About half a mile from the pier, another road
branched to the left. Their driver pulled up. "I
turn off here for the lighthouse. Just keep on
the main path," the driver said. "Take the first
branch to the right, it'll take you straight to the
fort."

"Let's get going," Frank said. "Those guys
aren't that far behind us."

"They're sure to see the pickup is empty
now—and this is the only way to go." Joe
pushed their pace to a jog.

The road skirted the lake and sank, turning
downright swampy. Some sections were more
mud than gravel. As they slogged along, they
could hear the sounds of the tide. "Great,"
Joe said. "We've got a lake on one side, and
what sounds like a cove on the other. All those
guys have to do is hang out here and we'll
never be able to get back past them."

"From the looks on their faces, I think we
can bet on their coming after us. Besides"—
Frank slapped at his neck—"if they stand still,
the mosquitoes might carry them off."

Joe slowed down for a second. "What if they

don't want to catch us?'' He turned to Frank. ''We came here to see if this is the fort Dundee meant. If it is, those guys could just be herding us to our slaughter.''

''I was wondering about that back on the truck,'' Frank admitted. ''But I don't think that mob was pretending to be in a sweat to catch us.'' He sighed. ''In fact, I think we may be heading for another dead end, but we've got to check it out.''

Joe gave his brother a quick look. ''Maybe you could find a better way to say that.''

The path began to lead uphill, then they reached the turnoff for the fort. The Hardys picked up the pace. Before their pursuers arrived, they had to investigate the fort and find a hiding place before circling back to the boat.

The path passed through a clump of trees, then opened out. A big sign read Parks Canada—Fort McNab—Danger.

''They got that right,'' Joe muttered as he looked around. He'd been expecting a smaller version of the Halifax Citadel—walls, defensive ditches, buildings, lots of hiding places.

Instead, the builders of Fort McNab had put up no walls at all. When Frank and Joe came out of the woods they were facing a hill, which was only broken here and there by huge, cement-walled rooms carved into its side.

''Bombproof storage,'' Frank said, peering

through a yawning hole where doors and windows had been. "This is where they probably kept the ammunition."

"Ammunition for what?" Joe stared around. "There's nothing here." Except for the dugouts, they were in the middle of nowhere—with nowhere to hide. Except the woods or around the back of the hill. But the thugs would be in the woods by now.

The road curved to their left, around the hill. So the boys hurried on, looking for a hiding place.

Reaching the far side of the hill, they came to a large open space, with three crescent-shaped concrete walls rising about six feet high.

"Gun emplacements," Frank said, chinning his way to the top of the wall. "I can see water down there—this must have been part of the harbor defenses. They could blow away any enemy ship from up here." He looked at the distant shore. "Right now, I wish we were over there."

Behind the first two gun positions was a concrete blockhouse built into the hillside. Frank shook his head as they jogged by. "Too open—nowhere to hide."

At the end of the path there were no more buildings—just a small collection of scattered gravestones. Joe looked at his brother. "A *real* dead end," he said.

Frank pretended not to hear that. "There's still one place we have to check out." He pointed to a pillbox rising on the crest of the slope.

They climbed to the top of the hill and saw a huge stretch of harbor. "This must have been where they aimed the guns," Joe said.

"Great view, but a lousy place to hide," Frank complained.

"Looks like this isn't the fort Dundee meant. And we've run out of places to hide," Joe said.

Frank was about to agree when he saw movement on the other side of the hill, back where the path came out of the woods. Their pursuers had finally caught up. "Down," he snapped at Joe.

Crouched in the tall grass, they counted seven guys, all toting guns. The turbaned leader and one of the others carried mini-Uzis.

"The gang's all here," Joe whispered. "What do we do now?"

Frank watched as the tracking party broke up. "Come on," he whispered. They slithered along until the old pillbox blocked them from sight, then Frank ran down the back of the hillside toward the abandoned blockhouse.

"We want to be lying down and ready when

the first guy comes around this curve," Frank said, pointing at the path. "They're all splitting up to search." He looked his brother in the eye. "We didn't do too well finding a hiding place—but how about grabbing a hostage?"

Moments later Joe lay motionless in the brush, the rank stink of weeds in his nose. He pinched his nostrils. This wasn't the time to sneeze.

They'd chosen their spot carefully—it left them hidden, with a clear view of the path. Now it was down to waiting.

They heard the crunch of footsteps on gravel. Please let him be alone, each boy prayed to himself.

The searcher rounded the curve—he *was* alone. He wore a striped shirt, had a deep tan, and carried a 9 mm Beretta in his right hand. The gun pointed at the ground. He was ambling as if he were on a picnic.

Frank and Joe both rose. This was their chance.

Joe's feet caught the guy in the back. The gunman flopped to the ground, but twisted around and raised his gun. Frank stomped his wrist, then kicked the gun away. Joe came down with a roundhouse right. The guy was out before he had time to yell.

Frank grabbed the gun while Joe dragged their prisoner out of sight behind the blockhouse. Now it all depended on timing. They had to cut down and across the hill before the rest of the seven made it around to their position at the back of the hill.

Just as the Hardys were starting off they heard a shout from quite near. The words didn't make sense—they were in some foreign language—but the message was clear. Someone had discovered that one of their men had disappeared.

The Hardys pulled their prisoner upright and dragged him around to the front of the hill. Now, if there wasn't a guard at the fort entrance . . .

Frank and Joe could hear shouting from the back of the hill now—loud, worried voices calling what was probably their captive's name. They were almost in the clear—the forest was only a few feet away and it would give them all the cover they'd need. But, no. One of the searchers must have backtracked, spotted them, and was now letting out a wild yell.

Frank pivoted and snapped off a shot that pinged against a concrete wall on one of the dugouts. The guy hit the dirt, still yelling.

"Let's hustle," Frank muttered. But their prisoner, who was awake now, did his best to hold them back. He dug in his heels as the boys yanked on his arms. "Look, stupid—"

Frank jammed the gun into the prisoner's side.

"No!" The bellow came from behind them. Frank glanced back to see that the pursuers had formed a line, all with weapons up and leveled straight at them. But they weren't shooting—their turbaned leader had shouted to hold their fire. Probably didn't want them hitting their guy.

The Hardys took off down the trail. This time their fear gave them superhuman strength, and their prisoner bounced easily between them.

But speed was impossible on the stones—either the small pebbles turned under their feet, or the mud slowed them. They could hear the crunch of shoes on the pebbles behind them.

"Don't know if we can beat them this way," Joe gasped. "Maybe we'd better take off for the woods."

"If we were alone." Frank glanced at the prisoner. "Couldn't manage him there."

For Joe, the escape was like a nightmare in which he had to run but his feet were stuck in glue. He plowed along, his head down, gripping the captive's right arm. Mosquitoes swarmed in his face. Just ahead, he heard a bird calling.

Then off to his right, in the woods, he heard the crackle of brush.

"They're circling around us," he said as

57

they stumbled down in the marshy part of the trail. "If they catch us where the island narrows . . ."

He didn't need to say any more.

The trio staggered a little faster, but Frank and Joe knew it was hopeless. The ambush was just ahead, any time, any place.

They had almost reached the shore of the lake when Frank saw the duck family he'd noticed earlier suddenly lift off from the water. What had scared them? Then, at the edge of the water behind a tree, he saw the telltale edge of a loud sports shirt.

"Joe," he whispered, nodding with his head.

Following Frank's eyes, Joe caught sight of the ambusher. He grinned. "Hold him here a second," he said, bending down to collect a few good-size stones.

He slipped off the path, skirting along the mucky edge of the lake. When he was behind the ambusher, he began hurling rocks at top speed.

The guy stepped back, lost his balance, and toppled into the lake with a splash.

Heads appeared from behind other trees, and Frank sent a couple of bullets whistling over their heads before dropping and taking cover.

The ambush disintegrated into wild shooting and shouting.

"Who's fooling with those blasted fireworks?" an angry voice demanded. From the turnoff leading to the lake stalked two angry tourists from the boat. "It nearly scared us to death."

Guns and ambushers disappeared at the first sign of witnesses. So did Frank, Joe, and the captive—straight for the dock.

Just before they emerged from the forest, Frank suddenly handed Joe the gun and pointed behind them. The prisoner turned to look—and when he did, Frank grabbed his neck, digging into two pressure points. The guy was out.

When the captain saw the Hardys carrying their new friend onto the boat, he asked what had happened to him.

"I don't know," Joe said.

The captain stood at the helm and steered the boat away from the dock. Frank sat beside the "patient" in the cockpit. The captive lolled in his seat, head down, hands dangling between his knees. Joe stood by the door, his eyes on the one stairway that led up to the deck they were on, his hand on the gun in his pocket.

"Captain," Frank said, "you may want to radio the Halifax police. This guy—"

Before he could finish the sentence, the prisoner bolted upright, slammed Frank to one side, and reached for his ankle. Then he was on his feet, four inches of gleaming knife blade in his hand.

"No radio," he said, threatening the captain with his knife. The guy spoke English all along. Then he turned to Joe. "You give me the gun."

Joe had the pistol in his hand, but there was no chance for a clear shot without endangering the captain or his brother. He stepped back out onto the sundeck. The prisoner grabbed the captain, using him for cover as he followed.

"The gun—before I lose patience."

His knife gleamed at the captain's throat now.

Joe had retreated all the way to the ship's rail. The escaped prisoner pursued, pushing the captain ahead of him.

"The gun," the man snarled.

Joe knew that once this guy had the pistol in his hand, it was all over. He had only one choice. . . .

Holding the gun out, he tossed it in a high arc over the rail and into the water below.

The thug's eyes followed the Beretta. And in that moment Joe's fist flashed out. He caught the guy in the side of the head, sending him staggering toward the rail. The captain batted his knife hand away, dodging in the opposite direction.

Before the guy could bring his knife up

again, Joe unleashed a sledgehammer right—
an uppercut that lifted his opponent high into
the air.

Then the guy tumbled back—over the rail
and into the waters of Halifax Harbor.

Chapter

8

"MAN OVERBOARD!" the captain shouted.

From the lower deck, Frank and Joe could hear running footfalls as crewmen and tourists dashed for life preservers.

They easily spotted the guy in the water by the brightly colored shirt he wore. He was floating facedown, the shirt billowing up and over his back. Frank and Joe watched as someone threw out a rope with a life preserver attached.

But the guy in the water didn't even make an attempt for it.

"Something's very wrong here," the captain said, slipping off his shoes and shirt. He dove into the water from the sundeck and swam over to the escaped prisoner. After hooking one arm around him and the other around the life preserver, he let the crew haul them back to the boat.

Frank and Joe ran down to the lower deck in time to help drag the limp form of the prisoner over the side. Laying him facedown, the crew brought his arms up over his head, trying to force any water from his lungs. Only a little came up.

"Let me," Frank said. "I know mouth-to-mouth."

The captain shouted to the pressing crowd, "Give us some room. We have the situation in hand." The tourists moved off.

Frank bent the guy's head back to open the breathing passage. Then he opened the man's mouth, took a deep breath, and pinching the guy's nose, leaned over to pump air into his lungs.

But before he reached the guy's mouth, he flinched and moved back, his eyes watering.

"What's the matter?" Joe demanded.

"He's dead," Frank said simply.

The captain knelt by the man, first feeling for a heartbeat, then for a pulse. "You're right," he said, abruptly standing. "Look at his lips."

Even as they watched, the man's lips were taking on a bluish tinge.

"Cyanosis—a typical indication of lack of oxygen," the captain said. He gave a half smile at Frank's surprised look. "During the school year I go to medical school."

He frowned down at the still form on the deck. "Get a blanket from inside the cabin to cover him up." Then he headed up the stairs, back to his cockpit. "I'd better get on the horn to the police."

His frowning gaze shifted from the body to Frank and Joe. "Shame about the poor guy," he said. "Drowning on such a small amount of water."

A crewman brought a blanket to cover the dead body. "What made you jump back like that?" Joe asked after he left.

"Something I smelled," Frank replied. "He was right about the cyanosis. But that guy didn't turn blue from lack of oxygen. I smelled cyanide on him."

Joe blinked. "Cyanide? You mean someone poisoned him?"

"Nope. I think he poisoned himself," Frank answered. "The smell seemed to come from around his mouth. He may have crushed a pill between his teeth."

"Come on," Joe said in disbelief. "The next thing you're going to tell me is that he's an Assassin." He shook his head and smiled at his brother.

The Hardys had crossed swords with the Assassins before, fighting desperate battles with these terrorists for hire. They'd thwarted an assassination attempt against a presidential candidate and an attempt to cut the Alaskan pipeline.

But those victories had come at a high cost. Iola Morton, Joe's first love, had disappeared in a fireball from an Assassin bomb, a bomb that had been meant for Frank and Joe.

Silence grew as Frank didn't answer his brother.

"I mean, let's get real," Joe said. "Assassins in Halifax?"

Frank shrugged. "You said the same thing about Assassins in Alaska," he said. "Think a minute. This guy follows their method of operation—he died rather than be captured and questioned."

They stood beside the covered form, silent for the twenty-minute ride back to Halifax.

It was dinnertime when the ferry docked, and since the boys were near, they headed for the Hungry Guardsman. Strange, they thought. There were no diners in the outdoor café area, and when Joe pushed against the door, it was locked.

Just as he was turning away, the door popped open, and the pert face of Shauna MacLaren appeared. "Sorry, we're closed—getting ready for a private party."

Then she recognized the Hardys. "Aren't you the guys who gave me a ten and left most of your dinners on the table last night?" she asked. "Are you hoping for a refund?" She grinned at Joe with a flirtatious look in her eye.

"Actually, we were hoping just to come in and finish a meal," Joe said. "But if you're closed—"

"Oh, come on in. I can make you a sandwich at least. I mean, we have a reputation to protect," she said, tossing the words over her shoulder on the way to the kitchen.

With sodas and two thick sandwiches of something called "smoked meat" in hand, Frank and Joe were soon sitting with Shauna in the empty restaurant. Most of the staff were still working in the kitchen, but she'd finished her chores.

They chatted for a few moments before Shauna asked, "So how do you like Halifax?"

The Hardys glanced at each other for a second, then Joe said, "It's not the easiest city we've ever visited." He went on to explain why they'd come there and what misadventures they'd had.

Shauna shook her head. "I heard about that

car exploding on the news. And you've been checking out forts ever since? I wonder if you met my friend Charlie Bell—he's a corporal in the Seventy-eighth this year. We go to school together.''

Her face grew more and more serious as she heard about the incident on the excursion boat. ''So you think he poisoned himself?'' She shuddered.

''What I don't understand is how they found us so quickly,'' Joe said. ''We changed hotels and didn't even get our luggage. When we started out today, we took a long walk, just to see if we did have a tail. And I'll swear we didn't.''

Frank nodded. ''I've been thinking about that, too. They couldn't just have picked up on us at the Citadel. There wouldn't have been time to rig that bomb. They had to have tailed us, or they just happened to see us at Fort Needham Park. And then they overheard our plan to go to the Citadel. It had to be that they just stumbled on us.''

Frank turned to Shauna, an idea forming. ''What's that area like?''

''By the park?'' Shauna asked. He nodded. She shrugged. ''I guess you'd say it was the poor side of town.''

''Well, that's where I think we should start looking.''

"For what?" Shauna wanted to know.

"Our attackers. Maybe their headquarters is *near* Fort Needham Park."

Frank looked down at his empty plate. "Whatever that sandwich was, it was great. Are you sure we shouldn't pay for it?"

"Just come back," Shauna said with a grin at Joe. "And, of course, tell all your friends."

Joe grinned back. "I don't know—the last time we brought people in here, they turned out to be pretty rough."

That got a laugh from Shauna.

Right then they were interrupted by a knock on the glass door. Shauna jumped up to answer it. A businessman in a blue suit and briefcase stood there.

"Sorry," Shauna said, shaking her head, "we're closed."

The man shouldered the door open, pointing to Frank and Joe. But Shauna just shook her head more determinedly. *"Closed,"* she said.

That seemed to get through. The man shrugged and set off down the street.

"Sometimes I have to be pretty firm." Shauna looked a little embarrassed, especially since Joe kept looking after the guy.

"There's something not right here," Joe said abruptly. "That guy left his briefcase right by the door."

Leaping up from his seat, he hustled them away from the door and windows—just in time.

The briefcase went up in a roar, filling the space where they'd been sitting with a hailstorm of jagged glass.

Chapter

9

THE BLAST NEARLY caught Frank, Joe, and Shauna in a part of the room that had been cleared for dancing. Joe managed to haul his brother and Shauna behind a table. Shards of broken glass rattled against it, points sticking into the wood.

Frank Hardy shook his head, his ears still ringing from the concussion. Then he began to hear the crackle of the flames. The wooden floor and tables by the door had caught on fire.

"We'd better get out of here," he said, getting to his feet.

"Out the back way!" Shauna grabbed Frank and Joe's arms, leading them away from the rapidly spreading fire.

The doors from the kitchen burst open, and a heavyset guy with a big bushy beard came charging up, holding a fire extinguisher. A quick look told Frank that wouldn't be enough to beat this blaze. He followed Joe and Shauna through the swinging doors and found himself confronting the whole kitchen staff.

"What's going on?" asked a young guy with carrot-colored hair. He wore an apron over jeans and a T-shirt and held a knife in his hand. Frank figured he must be an assistant cook.

"You wouldn't believe us if we told you," Shauna said.

"Have you called the fire department?" Frank asked.

The guy stared. "Why? Bob's out there with the fire extinguisher."

A moment later Bob came swinging back in through the doors, coughing his head off. "Too much," he gasped. "Call the fire—"

A blare of sirens cut him off. Someone else must have noticed the smoke.

"Out, out." Bob made shooing gestures, and the kitchen staff meekly headed out the rear door. Wisps of smoke were now coming through the thin gap between the swinging doors.

Frank and Joe followed Shauna out the door as the first wave of fire fighters arrived.

"Well," said Joe, "I don't think there'll be a party tonight."

Shauna nodded, a little forlorn. "Tonight— and quite a few other nights," she agreed. Then her face became furious looking. "Imagine the nerve of that guy! He could have killed us."

"I think that was the idea," Frank said a little dryly. Then to his brother he said, "Those other six guys must have sneaked back on the boat when we weren't looking."

Then his face grew even more serious. "Too bad we didn't get a look inside that case," he said. "I'd have liked to see if that bomb had a Fellawi loop."

"A who-what?" Shauna asked.

"My brother's a bomb buff," Joe told her. "He knows everybody's trademarks." More to Frank, he pointed out, "If you'd gone to take a look, the bomb would have blown up in your face."

Shauna poked them both. "So—what do we do now?"

Frank grinned. "That's usually Joe's line— and what do you mean, 'we'?"

"Well, these terrorists or whatever they are have just put me out of a job," she said. "It seems only fair that I should get a shot at revenge. Besides," she pointed out, "you really need someone who knows the town. Otherwise, you'll just waste more time looking at empty forts."

Frank looked at Joe. "Looks like we've got ourselves a native guide."

"A very *pretty* native guide." He turned to Shauna. "Okay, lead us to Fort Needham—a nice, confusing route, to give anybody following us a headache."

"Right." Shauna led them around the block, where an ancient stone facade hid an ultramodern hotel. She led them through the elegant lobby, past a row of shops, then up an escalator. They found themselves on another shopping arcade, with a walkway at the end leading to another building.

As they walked above the early evening traffic, Frank and Joe looked back to see if they could spot a tail. Nobody was there.

"I've seen a lot of these walkways downtown," Joe said. "Why do you use them instead of walking in the fresh air?"

"If you were here in the winter, you wouldn't ask," Shauna replied. "Besides, it beats climbing up and down hills, which isn't fun in ice and snow."

In the next building she led them through several shops and made a couple of unexpected turns, again to shake or isolate any tails. None showed up.

Shauna then took them out a back entrance,

around the mall, down several streets, three-quarters of the way around a churchyard, and then finally to Gottingen Street.

Joe shook his head in defeat. "If that didn't turn up anyone following us, I'd say we were in the clear."

"Right," said Frank. "Let's head for the park—and keep our eyes open."

They reached Fort Needham without seeing anything out of the ordinary. "I don't get it," Frank said, leaning against the strange bell tower on the bluff. His eyes bored out toward the harbor in the distance. "If they caught us once, why couldn't they catch us again?"

"Dumb luck?" Joe suggested, sitting on the grass to rest his feet. Shauna sat beside him.

"I don't like to credit things to luck," Frank said. "It's not logical, rational, or—I don't believe this!"

He stepped back against the cement of the bell tower, keeping out of someone's sight. "Joe," he said calmly, trying to keep the excitement out of his voice, "look who's here."

Easily—with no fast movements to catch anyone's attention—Joe rose to his feet. He turned as if he were talking to Shauna, then glanced over to where Frank was looking.

He couldn't believe his eyes. There, walking down a path in the park with the sun very low in the sky behind him, was their old pal, the guy in the turban. Now he was leaving the path and heading down a grassy slope to a side street.

From their position on top of the bluff, the Hardys and Shauna could see his course clearly.

"What do you think?" Joe said. "He didn't act like he saw us. He didn't act like he was looking for us. Maybe he's doing just what it looks like—maybe he's just cutting across the park."

"Or maybe," Frank said, "he's setting us up again. I'd hate to get locked up in a room with another bomb."

"I say we follow him." Joe started along the path, hands in his pockets, as if he were taking a stroll.

Mr. Mustache never looked back as the side street became a flight of stairs, leading down to the waterfront area.

"I wonder what he wants down by the dock?" Shauna said.

That end of the harbor didn't have the bustling energy they'd seen on piers on the rest of the waterfront. Railroad tracks, a warehouse or two, and what looked like a sheet-metal shop made up most of the landscape.

The building their quarry headed for was definitely a rundown warehouse. It took the three a little while to get close. The area was flat pavement, like a gigantic parking lot. They couldn't risk being seen by the turbaned man—even if he wasn't looking back.

Using what cover they could, they finally made it to the building. The door stood wide open.

"Shauna," Frank whispered, "you stay here as lookout. Give us a whistle if anyone comes along."

She nodded, taking a position by the corner of the building.

Frank and Joe stole inside. Dead ahead of them, across the vast room, were wide-open loading bays. No one was around. To their right were storage bays, with a hodgepodge of small-ish boxes, bales, and crates.

"So, can you tell me if the ship has finally been unloaded?" The voice came from a glassed-in office in the left corner of the floor. The Hardys didn't have to worry about being spotted—nobody had washed the glass in years.

Frank frowned. The voice had a trace of an accent. But he couldn't quite place it.

Joe and he darted for shelter behind some boxes when they heard the office door rattle.

"I knew it was important to you, Mr. Singh." A man in a stained jacket came out of the room, followed by the turbaned guy. "That's why I kept an eye out for it. Came in just this afternoon, so I kept it out special. You were lucky I decided to work late tonight."

The man stopped in the middle of the room to pat a long, bulky packing case. "See? She's right here. Pity you didn't bring your truck."

"Can I use your phone? I'll call for the truck."

"Fine, and then we'll go over the shipping papers."

Frank and Joe stayed low in the shadows as the two men headed back to the office.

As soon as the door was closed, they sneaked over to the crate. A shipping manifest was taped to the rough wood, along with a bill of lading.

Frank quickly scanned over entries like factor, port of embarkation, transshipment point, until— "Here it is—consignee. That's the person who's supposed to receive it."

He read the name typed beside the form entry. "Forte Brothers, Inc."

He raised an eyebrow at Joe. "I think we've found our fort."

Chapter

10

"BUT I'D LIKE to know what kind of presents these Forte Brothers are getting," Joe said. He looked around for a crowbar or anything to wedge the crate open.

Just then Shauna's whistle sounded from outside.

Joe dashed for the doorway, then back. "There're the lights of a car in the distance, and it seems to be heading this way."

Frank took off running for a corner of the warehouse, where he'd spotted a forklift truck. "Joe, start looking through those storage bays. We need a crate about the size and shape of this one."

While Joe darted down the alleyways of the

bays, Frank turned on the engine of the fork-lift. All this frantic action took place in nearly absolute silence. Joe's footfalls were smoth-ered by the rubber soles of his running shoes. And the forklift had an electric motor, which only gave off a low hum as Frank maneuvered it to the crate.

Frank lined up the blades of the forklift with the openings in the wooden skid under the box. It took him only a moment of fumbling to figure out how to lift the fork up so he could move the crate away. He quickly got the knack, and soon was trundling the crate to the back of a storage bay where Joe stood. Joe was beckon-ing frantically and pointing down the bay. Half-way down the alley was a crate nearly identical to the one Frank had just moved.

Frank dropped off his cargo and maneuvered in to pick up the new box. He whispered to Joe, "Go and take the papers off the crate—*carefully*. We don't want a torn packing slip making them suspicious when we put those papers on the new crate."

With the new crate secured on the forklift, Frank spun and drove out to the spot where the original crate had been. The car must be at the warehouse by now, and he hoped Shauna had sense enough to hide.

He carefully lowered the crate, disengaged the fork, and backed up. Joe ran over to the crate and smoothed on the papers he'd taken from the original crate.

Frank drove quickly to put the truck back where he'd found it. Just as he was jumping from the driver's seat, he heard the sound of a vehicle pulling up outside and the honk of a horn.

The office door opened, and Frank dove for cover behind the forklift.

Joe was out in the open, standing next to the crate. A good twenty feet of open space separated him from the nearest storage bay. Realizing he'd be seen if he made a run for it, he ducked down behind the crate.

The warehouse manager and Mr. Singh, as he was called, stepped out of the office. "These must be my people now," Singh said.

Joe held his breath. Would they notice anything odd? The forklift wasn't exactly where it had been. Neither was the crate. But the two men hardly gave the area a second glance.

Joe let out an inaudible sigh of relief as he heard their footsteps move away from him. He peeked around the side of the crate to see the backs of the two men heading for the warehouse door.

A van stood just outside, its doors open. This was the only chance he'd get. Rising to his feet, Joe darted noiselessly for the nearest bay—and safety. In seconds he had worked his way down an alley and found a nice pile of boxes to hide behind.

Frank had slipped from behind the forklift to find a hiding spot, too. He watched as Singh, the warehouse manager, and three other guys approached the crate in the center of the floor. The manager pawed around in his soiled jacket, finally coming up with a pen. "Sign here and here, and the shipment's yours."

He sighed. "Must be tough for the relatives to wait for it to come by boat. Pretty sad."

"Sadness is our business," Singh replied. "And it was a monetary decision for them. Air freight is so very expensive."

The manager was still shaking his head as he walked over to the forklift. He turned it on, then expertly whipped it around, bringing it over to the crate. "Better move your van to the loading dock," he said. "It'll be easier."

The manager then drove the forklift and its burden over to the open side of the warehouse. He was silhouetted against the darkening sky, easing the machine down to the end of the loading bay.

The van backed up to the dock, then Singh and one of the other guys stepped out of the back doors, carrying something between them. Neither Frank nor Joe could see it clearly. But it seemed to be a collapsible metal frame on wheels.

They set it up on the floor of the bay. Several grunts later, they had the box on their collapsible stretcher and wheeled it into their van.

Singh waved goodbye to the manager, then he took off.

After driving the forklift back to the far wall, the warehouse manager strolled back to his office.

Joe could hardly wait for him to close the door. He'd found a crowbar, and he was itching to get the top off the mystery crate. He popped out of his hiding place.

Frank appeared, too, and headed past Joe to the door. "I'm going to tell Shauna what's going on," he whispered. "She's probably getting worried out there."

"Uh, right," Joe agreed. He tapped the crowbar in his open palm. "Well, I'll get started on the crate."

"Just do it quietly," Frank said. "Any sound of splintering wood will bring our friend out."

As if on cue, a muffled noise came from inside the office—the sounds of a war. Joe grinned as he heard a cavalry bugle, gunshots, and war cries. "He must have a TV in there," he said. "As long as the shooting keeps up, we can afford a little noise."

Nothing appeared to be stirring outside— then Frank caught a flicker of movement. It was Shauna, peeking round the corner of the building.

"Frank!" she gasped. "I didn't know what had happened to you."

"We pulled a switcheroo," he explained to her. "The box they left with wasn't the box they came for."

"Where's Joe?" Shauna wanted to know.

"Inside, opening the real crate. We want to know what these guys were supposed to get."

Curious, Shauna started toward the door. Frank gently took her arm to stop her. "We need you out here still. Our box isn't going to fool those guys very long—just till they open it up. Keep an eye out for them. As soon as you see them coming, warn us. Okay?"

Shauna pouted for only a second but then had to admit that Frank was right. "But I want a blow-by-blow description," she warned.

Frank grinned. "Joe has an instant camera. He'll take pictures."

He went back inside to bring his brother up to date. Joe had loosened all the nails on three sides of the box, and was working on the last one. He chuckled when Frank told him of his promise. "Well, I've got the camera right here," he said, touching a pocket in his summer-weight jacket. "I suppose we'll need the evidence, anyway."

Joe pried up the last of the nails, then silently

pulled the lid of the crate free. He propped the lid against a pile of boxes, then turned back to watch Frank burrow through packing material.

"So, what is it?" Joe asked.

Frank had finally scooped enough of the packing stuff out of the way and stared down.

"Would you believe a coffin?" he asked.

Chapter

11

FRANK AND JOE both leaned in and began sweeping the packing material out with their arms. Together, they cleaned off the whole top, creating a snowstorm of polystyrene peanuts.

The box inside the crate was dull silver in color, about seven feet long and three feet wide. The top was in two sections, with a hairline crack between them.

As he stared down at the grim-looking shape, Joe Hardy had to admit that his brother's first guess was right. They were looking at a coffin.

"Well, this explains what Singh was talking about," Frank said. "Remember when he was talking with the manager? He said something like, 'Sadness is our business.'"

Joe nodded. "Yeah. I guess if we looked up Forte Brothers in the phone book we'd find out that they're funeral directors."

"Probably," Frank agreed. He stared at the coffin for a moment, poked against the top, and then looked over at his brother. "You have your Swiss army knife? I need a screwdriver."

"What do you need a screwdriver for?" Joe asked. Then, when he figured it out, he looked at Frank's determined face, appalled. "Oh, no," he said. "Wait a minute. You're not going to open this thing, are you?"

"Just the top half," Frank admitted.

Joe stared. "You've finally lost it completely. We *know* what's in there. Who are you expecting to find, Count Dracula?"

"We don't *know* what's in there," Frank replied. "But I think we ought to find out." He held out his hand for the knife.

Joe Hardy finally dug it out and handed it over. "This coffin has spent *weeks* on some freighter," he said. "Remember what the manager said about the relatives waiting. Are you sure you want to open it? I mean, after all, what would you expect someone to ship to a funeral parlor?"

"You're forgetting that these guys aren't normal funeral directors." Frank bent over and reached under the sides of the coffin, feeling for the screws that held the top closed. "They shoot guns and leave bombs around. That's not normal—unless Halifax has a shortage of dead people and they're drumming up business.''

"It all sounds weird to me." Joe shook his head in disbelief.

"No, it all makes a horrible kind of sense," Frank insisted as he worked on the screws. "A phony funeral home would be a perfect cover. I mean, who would bother a mortician? And if he has the odd body to get rid of, it couldn't be easier—''

He grunted as a tight screw resisted him for a second. "And if you were smuggling things into a country, what better way than in a coffin? Who'd check it out?" A little more work, then Frank straightened up suddenly. "That's it. The top should lift off."

Joe stepped away from the coffin. "What if you're wrong? This could be pretty gross." He shuddered. "Horrible, I mean."

"Don't be silly." Still, Frank took a deep breath before he swung the top open.

He looked in and quickly shut the lid. The coffin wasn't empty—it did contain a body.

"See, I told you, "Joe said.

But Frank slowly eased the lid up again for another look. This time he reached in and dug his fingernail into the face of the body.

"Have you gone crazy?" Joe said louder than he'd intended.

"Nope. And this isn't skin under my nail. It's wax. At first glance the dummy looks real, but it's made of wax."

When he pulled down the blanket covering the body, Frank found a little door in the left-hand side of its chest. Joe stared. The door was right where the heart would be on a living person.

"This poor guy isn't getting a very comfortable final rest." Joe tried a joke to cover up for his earlier nervousness. "I thought most coffins had padded silk linings. Look at this." He ran a finger along the dull, grayish black metal that lined the box. His fingernail scratched a line in it. "What is this stuff, anyway?"

Frank scratched at it, too, managing to break a thin piece off. "Lead foil, I think." He frowned, then quickly tossed the piece back into the coffin.

Meanwhile, Joe had pulled his camera out of his pocket. "I guess we ought to take some pictures," he said. "What do you think? Full face or profile? Should we shoot him lying down or sitting up?" he asked, his sense of humor returning.

Frank bent down, reaching across the coffin to the dummy's left side. "At least we should take out whatever's inside."

He hesitated a second. Something very unpleasant could be hidden inside the dummy.

Then he braced himself, grabbed the little handle on the door, and pulled.

"Huh!" Joe said, disappointed. "I thought we'd find jewels or something. But that—I don't even know what that is."

Tucked deep inside the cavity in the dummy's chest was a small metal cylinder, maybe two inches high and one inch wide. The outside was highly polished.

"Looks like stainless steel," Joe said. "I don't see any openings. Maybe it twists apart." He set his camera down on the dummy's chest and started to reach into the opening for the mysterious metal container.

Frank's hand moved like a striking snake, clamping on to Joe's wrist. "Don't touch it," he said.

Joe twisted in surprise and dropped his little instant camera into the opening. "Okay," he said. "Could I at least take a picture?"

He snatched up the instant camera and stepped back to snap the coffin, its strange inhabitant, and the bizarre opening with its mysterious cargo.

"Now don't move," he said playfully, his finger going for the shutter release. But he never took the picture.

"Hey, guys."

Joe turned at the sound of running feet.

Shauna was peering down the shadowy loading bay, trying to find them.

"Over here," Frank said.

She froze when she got close enough to see what they were bending over. Shauna stared for a second, then pulled herself together. "We've got to get out of here," she said.

Frank glanced toward the door. "They're back?"

Shauna nodded. "With reinforcements, it looks like. There's another set of lights behind the van's. And they're both driving like maniacs."

Frank slapped down the little door in the dummy's chest, then closed the top of the coffin.

He turned to pick up the wooden lid for the crate, then shook his head. "We don't have time to hide our tracks. Let's just get out."

The three of them turned and were dashing for the loading docks just as squealing brakes and angry horns announced the arrival of Singh and his men.

Chapter

12

FRANK, JOE, AND Shauna jumped from the loading dock down to the bay, where they'd be less likely to be seen.

Crouched down, they made their way toward the edge of the building. The sooner they put a brick wall between themselves and the uproar going on behind them, the better.

Leaning against the wall, Frank could hear Singh yelling and screaming at the warehouse manager. The poor manager, of course, couldn't understand the mix-up. At least six other voices joined in the shouting.

Then the voices split up, accompanied by lots of banging and crashing. "Sounds like they've decided to search the place," Frank said. "Let's get out of here while they're still busy."

With the warehouse behind them, they tried to figure an escape route. To their right was the harbor itself, to their left the bluffs that cut the dock off from the rest of the city. At the top of the bluffs was a heavily traveled street. But getting there wouldn't be easy. The wide-open spaces around the warehouse would make them easy targets even in the dark.

In the near distance rose a redbrick warehouse, with the name "Collins" in white letters over the well-lit door. In between them and the brick warehouse were a couple of old freight cars on a railroad siding. That was it for cover. They'd be as exposed as a bug on a clean tablecloth if they made a run for it. But it was their only choice.

The yelling inside the warehouse went up another notch. "They must have found the coffin," Joe said.

Frank started out for one of the freight cars. "Come on! They'll be looking for us in a minute. We have to be out of direct sight by then."

By the time they'd darted behind the first freight car, they could hear a car engine turn over. "I don't know how you expect us to outrun a car," Shauna said.

Frank didn't answer. He was calculating

their chances of making it to the next piece of cover.

About thirty feet on was an old piece of machinery that had been blocked by the freight car. The question was, could they reach it before the searchers got that far in their car?

He looked at Joe, who shrugged. "Let's go for it."

They took off, Joe in the lead, Shauna following, Frank bringing up the rear. About halfway to their goal, they heard the whine of an engine and the screech of tires.

A compact car was zooming up directly at them.

"You guys keep going," Frank said. "I'll try to get them off your backs."

Joe knew what Frank was up to. He took Shauna's hand, leading her in a wild dash to the far side of the rusted machinery.

Frank ran for the near side, staying out in the open. He'd seen what he wanted in the headlight beams—a metal bar sticking out of the side of the decaying mass. Once it had been a controlling lever, but now it was just a foot-long piece of garbage, held on by rust.

As Frank ran past, he grabbed the bar and heaved. It came off almost too easily, making him stumble.

The car veered after him. As it approached, Frank was caught in the glare from its headlights. He swung around, whipping the metal bar at the car.

His weapon flew true, working even better than he'd expected. It shuddered along the car's hood, leaving a long, jagged scratch, and then it smacked into the windshield, cracking it into a hundred tiny lines.

The little car veered wildly as the driver screamed something. Frank grinned. The guy jammed on the brakes, actually stopping the car so he could lean out the window to take a shot at Frank.

While the driver's friend hauled him back in, Frank tried to increase the distance between them.

In the meantime, Joe and Shauna were running for the warehouse. It was up to Frank to keep the bad guys' attention on himself so they could make it.

The driver was back in the car now, and he had only one thing in mind—to run Frank Hardy down. The scary thing was, his aim was good.

The little car's engine was gunned, and suddenly it seemed to roar at twice its size.

Fortunately, Frank had a better turning radius than it had. He jumped to the side, and started running back to the rusted-out machinery.

The driver jammed on the brakes, sent the

car spinning wildly in a tight turn, and came after him again. Apparently, he wanted to turn Frank into a large oil spot on the pavement.

Frank dodged again, away from the machinery this time, but the car plowed on in a straight line. The driver had misjudged the angles a little. His right fender caught and scraped on the rusted mass, letting out a hideous screech.

Frank paid no attention, running for a trailer someone had parked beside the redbrick warehouse. It would give Frank lots of room to maneuver and hide behind—if he lived to make it there.

Behind him, Frank heard the car scream to life again, and the driver continued his game of cat and mouse. He was sure to blow out his engine if he kept driving that way. Maybe, though, the driver felt that would be okay, if he could just run Frank down.

Legs pumping, Frank risked a look over his shoulder. The car was aimed straight at him. He looked ahead. That trailer was too far— Frank knew he couldn't outrun the little monster. He'd have to dodge. Last time, he'd dodged left. This time he'd go right.

From the sound, Frank knew the car had blown its muffler. It now sounded like a racing machine as it thundered on. Frank glanced back again. How could he have thought of that car as small? It was huge—and only twenty feet behind him!

He faked left, then dove right. The driver hooked his car left, missed Frank, and went into a hair-raising skid as he jammed on the brakes and his wheels locked.

Frank leapt to his feet and ran like a maniac. The car was now in a position to cut him off. All that mistreatment must be affecting the car's handling, Frank hoped.

He refused to look at the car, concentrating only on the trailer ahead. But his side vision caught the movement of the car. It was zooming straight for him.

He stepped into a pothole he couldn't see because it was so dark and he fell.

It was a lucky fall. If he'd gone two steps farther, he'd have been right in the path of the speeding car.

It fishtailed through another crazy U-turn to come back. Frank had barely enough time to get up and throw himself to safety under the trailer before the car flew past him again.

This time, instead of screaming into another turn, the car screeched to a jerky stop, and two guys got out. Frank wondered if they really wanted to catch him or if they were just afraid of their friend's driving.

Well, he couldn't stay there and let the ground troops drive him out of cover. While the guys were still getting out of the car, Frank sprinted for the warehouse.

This building was long and thin—a rectangle—with loading bays on both sides. As he ran for the nearest bay, Frank could see straight through the building to the other side. The perfect short-cut—provided the two goons didn't station themselves on the far side.

He heard the car spin its wheels, but he knew he had it beat to the warehouse. Catching a ragged breath, Frank threw himself at the nearest loading dock—and nearly went into shock as a pair of strong arms gripped him.

Joe grinned down at him. "I thought you'd done enough," he said, walking into the warehouse with Frank. "While you kept those clowns occupied, I managed to get Shauna all the way over to the bluffs. There's a sort of path up there, and this bozo won't be able to drive after us. I guess we're lucky they didn't know at the warehouse what we did. They had to split up to search for us. Speaking of which"—he pointed to the bays on the far side of the building—"those goons plan to catch you as soon as you go out over there."

His grin got wider. "But they won't be expecting two of us, and I'm rested, so I can take the heat from the driver for a while." He led the way across the warehouse floor. "I have a plan."

Joe was right—the two guys weren't expecting two people to come out of the warehouse. Guns in hand, they'd positioned themselves at either end of the building, so that if Frank came for one, the other could cover him. When an attacker leapt on both of them, however, they weren't ready.

Frank jumped on his guy from the loading dock. The gunman dropped like a sack of potatoes. Joe had his man pinned to the ground, grappling with him. He gestured with his head for Frank to get going.

As Frank ran, he heard the sound of the compact car's engine laboring around the warehouse building. This was bad. There was no place to hide at all—just a few stunted weed-trees, and beyond them, railroad tracks. The tracks could throw the car out of control if it hit them, but that wouldn't stop the driver from going for *him*.

Then, as the car swerved around to aim for Frank, two shots rang out. He turned back and saw Joe smashing his adversary's gun hand against the ground.

Frank couldn't believe it. One bullet had taken out the car's left headlight, the other, the left front tire.

The driver had a new target now. His car barreled at Joe, who jumped safely aside. The driver came close to hitting his own man, who now lay out of it on the ground.

Joe got up and trotted, tauntingly slow, toward the far end of the building. It took the driver a little longer to take his battered car through the turnaround. But when he saw Joe almost reach the corner of the building, he floored the gas pedal to get him.

The car shimmied wildly but moved as fast as a rocket. Joe pretended to be unaware that it was coming, as he strolled toward the corner.

But when Joe did turn and saw the car, a look of horror crossed his face. He'd made his move too late. Even if he got around the corner, the driver could cut him down.

Joe raced around the corner and flattened himself against the building as the little car pursued him on two wheels.

The car slammed into a telephone pole. It shuddered and fell down right on the hood of the car.

That ended the chase.

The steep climb up the overgrown path wasn't easy, but Frank, Joe, and Shauna handled it quickly. They didn't want to be hanging around when their pursuers regained consciousness.

Shauna found a pay phone to call the police to report the accident. If those guys needed any help, they'd get it. In the meantime, they hoped, the police would keep them off the streets for a while.

"Where to?" Joe asked.

"Back to Fort Needham for a moment," Frank said.

"But it's dark," Joe said.

"It's lit up at night and looks very beautiful," Shauna said.

"I just want someplace pleasant where I can think," Frank replied. While he'd been busy escaping and running for his life, he hadn't had a chance to put together all the things he'd seen. Now . . .

Frank sat on the grass, smiling as Joe shot a flash picture of Shauna with his camera. Joe frowned at the result.

"Look at this," he complained. "The picture's all foggy—as if it had already been exposed. What do you think, Frank? Is it bad film? Or did I break the cam—"

Joe broke off when he saw Frank looking at the film as if it were a nightmare come true. "Come on, it's just a bad picture."

"Take another one," Frank ordered him. "Just shoot—anything."

Shrugging at Frank's weird reaction, Joe took another picture of Shauna. It was just as foggy as the first.

"This isn't a new load of film, is it?" Frank sounded as if he were interrogating Joe. "You took a perfectly clear shot of me in the air-port."

"It's the same film," Joe said. "What's the big deal?"

"I know how the film got ruined," Frank said. "Remember how the camera fell on that little metal canister inside the dummy? That's what did it."

"Did what?" Shauna asked.

"It irradiated the film." Frank looked at them with growing horror in his eyes. "That metal slug had a little pellet of something very radioactive inside. That's why those guys were so upset when we opened up the coffin and found it."

His voice dropped lower as he stared at the ruined prints. "We just saw a piece of an atomic bomb."

Chapter

13

"AN ATOMIC BOMB?" Shauna said, stumbling over the words in disbelief. "Here in Halifax? You must be joking."

Frank shook his head, ice growing in his stomach. "Actually, it makes a terrible sort of sense. Halifax is a big port city, with lots of ships—and people—passing through from all over the world. It's a Canadian city, a perfect place for the Assassins to launch a plot against the U.S. And there are three thousand miles of friendly border to smuggle it across—unless they bring it down by boat."

He looked slowly from the pictures to Shauna. "In fact, I couldn't think of a better place on the East Coast to assemble and build a nuclear bomb.''

She stared at him in complete shock. ''Well—we've got to do something about it! Tell the government! Tell the police!''

Joe sighed deeply. ''We can try,'' he said.

''*Try?*'' Shauna burst out.

''I think what Joe is trying to say is that we don't have much hard proof,'' Frank explained. ''A lot of things have happened— bombs going off, people getting hurt, even killed. But the police would have to take our word to pull it all together.''

''And cops aren't exactly eager to take a kid's word about something like this,'' Joe finished up for him. ''They think we get weird ideas from watching too many spy movies and just tune us out.''

Joe shook his head. ''The one contact we had on the force was Gerry Dundee. He found out something fishy was going on at Forte Brothers, and they shut his mouth for him.''

''We played it very straight, telling the police everything that happened since we arrived in town,'' Frank said. ''And the detective in charge just shrugged it off.''

''Think how he'd react if we came in and told him that his case ties in with some kind of nuclear terrorism plot.'' Joe's lips were a hard, thin line.

"But this is important!" Shauna wailed.

"Think about it for a minute," Joe said gently. "If you hadn't been along with us and we told you this story, would *you* believe it?"

"I . . . well, I would—" Finally, Shauna nodded. "I would think you were out of your minds. Back at the Hungry Guardsman, when you first started telling me all this stuff, I thought you were pulling my leg. Then that guy tried to blow the place up!"

Frank smiled. "Explosions are usually a good way to persuade people. But I'm afraid we can't depend on somebody planting a bomb at police headquarters when we go to talk to them." His smile faded. "We need some proof—something a lot stronger than foggy pictures and a story about a coffin. They won't go for a search warrant unless we have some solid proof."

"Luckily, we don't need search warrants— and we know where to find some proof." Joe began pacing back and forth. "So, where do the Forte Brothers do business?"

"I couldn't tell you that," Shauna said, heading out of the park. "But I'll lead you to the nearest phone book."

They found a telephone directory at a corner café a few blocks down from Fort Needham Park.

"Here it is," Shauna said, paging through

the directory. "It's about nine blocks from here, back the way we came, in the Hydrostone."

"The whozie-stone?" Joe asked.

"You know those houses behind Fort Needham Park?" Shauna said.

Frank and Joe nodded.

"It's a housing project," Shauna explained, "built in an area that was completely devastated. Hydrostone is a kind of concrete block—that's what they used to build the houses."

"Well, what do you say we head back there?" Joe said.

The others nodded. "But first I have to pick up a couple of things back at the hotel," Frank said.

Walking down the street that was listed as the address of Forte Brothers, they passed a line of closed and dark shops. The funeral home was in the middle of the block. No lights showed in the windows or on its porch.

Frank led the way to the end of the block and made a right. "There's too much street traffic to go in the front," he said. "Let's see how the back looks."

Joe had been expecting that. "It's the fourth house from the end. We'll just count our way up."

The stores backed up on a spacious alleyway, which they shared with the rear of a line of houses.

"Not as crowded," Frank muttered. "But we'll have to be quiet, unless we want the neighbors looking over our shoulders."

From the windows of one house, they could hear the theme music of a popular TV show.

"I think they've got other things to watch than us," Joe said.

"Let's hope so," Frank muttered, "because we're going in."

It turned out that they didn't need to count houses. Parked behind Forte Brothers was a dead giveaway—the company hearse. They hid behind it as they made their way up to the back door.

Frank slid the screen door open, bracing it with his knee. Then he knelt by the doorknob, slipping a little box with wires out of his pocket.

Shauna watched wide-eyed. "What's that?" she asked.

"It started out as a circuit tester. I made a few modifications." Frank touched the wires to the doorknob, then ran them up and down the space between the door and the frame. A light flashed on the box.

"Trouble," Frank whispered. "They've got an alarm on the door. Open it up, and a siren sounds."

"Does this mean we can't get in?" Shauna asked.

"It means we use the door as a last resort," Joe explained. He backed up to check the windows.

"Frank, look at the last window on the right—the one behind the bush."

Frank slid over, reached up, and felt around. "Bathroom window," he whispered. "We're in luck. Somebody left it open." Even so, he checked carefully for pressure pads or contacts in the window frame before he shoved the window up.

Then he switched on a miniflashlight, and shielding it with his hand, checked the tiled windowsill.

"People have a bad habit of leaving things on bathroom windowsills," Joe explained to Shauna. "If we knocked anything over coming in, it would land on the tile floor with a nice, loud crash."

"You think there still could be people inside?" She stared up at the dark windows.

"We don't know. So we'll play it safe."

Frank was leaning in the window now, playing his light around the room. He wasn't shielding it anymore. "The door's closed. I'm going in."

The creeping bush that grew up past the

window made the opening quite small, but Frank swung himself in.

Joe laced his fingers together to make a cup of his hands. "Put your foot in here," he told Shauna. "You're next."

With a boost from Joe, she made it in silently. Then Joe had to squeeze in.

He pulled out his own flashlight and glanced around the room. "Doesn't look like they're hiding the bomb in here," he whispered. "Where do we go next?"

Frank glanced back. "Kill the light." He stood with his ear to the door, listening. When he was sure no one was outside, he turned the doorknob and eased the door open. It made the slightest squeak, but no one came to investigate.

The hallway outside was carpeted—they could tell that much by feel. It was also totally dark. Frank and Joe flashed their lights in opposite directions. They saw a small sitting room by the front door, and two funeral chapels, one large, one smaller.

Joe also found a stairway with a small arrow pointing down and a sign that said Office.

"Let's check it out," Frank whispered.

At the foot of the stairs was a small, walled-in area with a door marked Private. Beyond that was a large, shadowy open area.

They tried the office first. It was a mess.

Piles of paper rose in one corner of the room. Frank went to check them, and they turned out to be nothing more than the business records of the firm. On top of the pile was a contract stating that the Forte Brothers had sold their business to somebody named Jihan Singh. He wondered if that was the Indian equivalent of John Smith.

Joe, in the meantime, was concentrating on a desk, which was littered with wires and tools. He touched a soldering iron, some resistors, and a digital timer, which he held up. "Look familiar?" he asked.

"I seem to remember disassembling something rather like that," Frank admitted. He flashed his light around. "This might be the workbench, but I don't see the finished product in here."

They stepped out of the office and into the larger space. As they flashed their lights around, they saw it was a salesroom. Racks lined the walls, with various styles of coffins on display.

Joe gave a low whistle. "I don't believe this," he said.

In the center of the room was what must have been the Cadillac of coffins. It was a metallic box about half the size of a luxury car and colored a carefully polished deep bronze.

The handles looked like solid gold, and probably cost as much as any three other caskets.

But unlike any of the other caskets, this one was closed. All the rest of the models were open.

Frank had a weird feeling the moment he saw this behemoth. He was stepping toward it, reaching out with his hand, when the lights suddenly snapped on.

Jihan Singh's voice rang out in the small room.

"It wouldn't be wise to touch that, Frank Hardy. There are conventional dangers as well as a nuclear one."

Chapter

14

SINGH WAS NOT alone. At least four other guys backed him up, all of them pointing Uzis or MAC-10 submachine guns at Shauna and the Hardys.

"How did you know we were here?" Joe asked, not caring about the firepower trained on him.

Singh smiled at him. "I'm surprised that you didn't notice the motion detectors. Each room has one. But, my dear Joe—you don't mind that I call you Joe?—we were *expecting* you." His smile got wider and brighter under his huge black mustache. "Why do you think we left that window open?"

Frank and Joe looked at each other, feeling like perfect chumps.

"So, now we have the famous Frank and Joe Hardy, and a lovely friend." Singh turned to Shauna. "Tell me, are you with the Halifax police? We know most of the local undercover forces. Or perhaps you represent the national forces? RCMP, perhaps."

"RCMP?" said Joe.

"Royal Canadian Mounted Police," Frank explained. "They handle a lot of security jobs—like the FBI back home."

Joe stared at the head terrorist. "You think she's a cop?" he asked in disbelief. "She's Shauna MacLaren, an architecture student and part-time waitress. One of your boys nearly blew her up when you planted that bomb at the Hungry Guardsman."

"Is this true?"

Shauna nodded, still staring silently at the four gun muzzles.

Singh nodded. "We worried that you might have gone to the authorities—especially when that unmarked police car came for you at Dartmouth. I had to use a local operative there who did not recognize Sergeant Dundee. But he did not know that his superiors no longer listened to the old man."

"Oh, yeah?" Joe said. "That 'old man' was the one who put us on to you."

"I knew he had started to ask some embarrassing questions." Singh shook his head. "He should have died of a heart attack, a stroke—something appropriate for a man his age. I'm afraid that bomb drew far too much attention."

"Why *have* you been trying to blow us up?" Frank demanded. "Ever since we arrived in this city—"

"Ever since I saw you arrive," Singh corrected. He stared at the Hardys. "You really don't know? Then, Frank and Joe, let me tell you about your rare honor—"

"You make it sound like 'This Is Your Life,' " Joe cut in.

Singh ignored him. "It's something the Assassins haven't used in nearly a hundred years. We've been ordered to kill you on sight."

The Hardys stared for a moment. Then Joe said, "Pretty heavy-duty. So you sicced your goons on us."

"Yes," Singh said. "You've been rather a drain on my local manpower. We have one dead, and three in local hospitals at this time. One is in the same Intensive Care Unit as is your friend Dundee. Luckily, none of these patients know the exact timing of our project."

"What's your rush?" Joe asked.

"It's *your* fault," Singh told him. "This is what you Americans call a crash project. I had just assembled my team when one of our most important agents was captured.''

"Captured? I thought all you people would die to avoid that," Joe taunted.

"It was very bad luck," Singh admitted.

Frank, however, was staring at the head Assassin with slitted eyes. "Who was this agent?"

"His code name is Adyab. You knew him as Sandy White.''

Sandy White led the Assassin task force working undercover to destroy the Alaska pipeline. During the *Trouble in the Pipeline* case, the Assassins almost succeeded in cutting the oil flow—except for Frank and Joe. In fact, Joe was the reason White had been captured. He'd literally punched the poison tooth out of White's mouth.

"We have word that Adyab is still resisting interrogation," Singh told them. "But for how much longer? He knows too many damaging facts about our organization. We can't allow him to be cracked.''

"So you're going to take an entire city hostage," Frank said.

Singh nodded. "You live up to your reputation for having a quick mind," he said. "My project was pushed ahead as having the best chance of getting Adyab released.''

"Well, it certainly raises the stakes," Frank

admitted. "You must have had a pretty tough job."

"With an international organization, much can be accomplished," Singh said. "We had already begun collecting fissionable material. I had a physicist for the theoretical design. All I needed was an explosives expert."

"And you got Omar Fellawi."

"You recognized his work." Singh smiled at Frank. "He was most impressed that you survived. I'll introduce you in a moment—after we make sure you can't cause trouble."

He gestured to a row of heavy metal caskets. "Please back up against them." Then he pulled sets of handcuffs out of his pocket.

Joe glanced at Frank. This might be the only chance they'd get to make a move.

But Singh was too experienced to fall into any traps. As his prisoners moved, so did the guards, keeping them covered at all times. And he was careful to stay out of the line of fire as he cuffed Frank, Joe, and Shauna. Not only were their hands behind their backs, but the chains between their cuffs ran through a handle on each of the three different coffins.

"It's just a small precaution to keep you from moving around," he said. "And don't bother screaming for help. This room is sound-proofed. One of the first improvements I made after buying the place. It makes an excellent safe house, doesn't it?''

"Very clever," Frank said, complimenting him.

"My plan was well along, except for the problem of getting the nuclear materials into the city. Then I had the idea—''

Singh looked at Frank. "You may be aware of the sudden outbreak of terror in the Middle East?''

"I've been reading about it, yes.''

"But have you noticed the number of Canadians who've recently lost their lives? There was one in that bus who blew up, another on that boat.''

Frank looked hard at the terrorist. "Now that you mention it, there have been quite a few.''

"Six, to be exact—six paper people that I created. Passports, tickets, visas, I arranged for them all. Then I gave them to agents who traveled under the identities. Since we knew where and when these—disasters were to occur, it was easy enough to plant the identification papers. Then other friends and agents took care of sending back the 'remains.' Of course, you saw what was really shipped.''

Frank nodded. "Dummies in lead-lined coffins, each carrying a slug of—what? Uranium? Plutonium?''

"Uranium-238," a new voice cut in. A short, thickset man thumped down the steps on stumpy legs. His coarse blond hair was shaved down to a brush cut, and his icy blue eyes crackled with intelligence. "Six slugs—sixty grams. Less than an ounce of fissionable material, but enough to make two nuclear bombs."

"Thank you, Herr Professor," Singh said. "Let me introduce Ranulf Lupec, our scientific advisor."

"So these are the people who kept you so busy these last few days?" There was the faintest trace of an accent in Lupec's words as he looked at the prisoners. He could just as easily have been examining a shipment of laboratory rats.

Another figure came down the stairs—a tall, gawky guy with a beak of a nose, wild black hair, and a receding hairline. He looked like the kind of person who wound up running the soda machine in a fast-food joint. Yet Frank found himself looking at the man's hands. The fingertips were stained with nicotine and acid. But the long, thin fingers were amazingly graceful, even grasping a heavy lead box.

"Omar Fellawi?" Frank asked.

The lanky man stopped and gave him a big grin. "You are the one who took apart my bomb," he said. "Very smart—I must stop using that loop."

He turned away to the coffin in the center of the room. "I would like to talk, but there is work to finish."

Frank watched as Fellawi ran his fingers over several places on the casket—on one of the locking bolts, behind a handle, and at the base. Then he carefully swung the coffin lid open.

Even the hardened killers shrank back; only Lupec, Singh, and Fellawi leaned over the revealed machinery.

"This is a gun-type atomic weapon." Lupec spoke to the prisoners almost as if he were lecturing a class. "An explosive charge drives a small piece of uranium into a larger piece at two thousand feet per second. When the two pieces are smashed together, they reach critical mass and explode with the force of thousands of tons of dynamite."

He smiled. "It's the simplest form of bomb. The Americans were so sure of this design, they didn't even test it before dropping it on Hiroshima."

"Yes, the design is simple," Fellawi said. "Making it work—*that* is hard. Especially when these young people try to steal our parts."

"The slug you tried to intercept was our final shipment," Singh explained.

"We didn't try to intercept anything," Joe told him. "We didn't even know what it was until after we left."

Frank had been thinking over something else Lupec had said. "You said you'd smuggled in enough for two bombs," he began.

"That's right," Singh told him. "We have the assembly for one bomb all ready to be brought across the border. Omar here is finishing our second one right now."

Fellawi had opened up the lead box and removed a short, fat cylinder, maybe four inches tall. He bent over the innards of the coffin-bomb and began working with his magic fingers. "I move it here, I shift here, slip it in— good. Now, I make the connections." He looked around. "Where is my soldering iron?"

A guard dashed into the office and came back with the tool. Fellawi leaned over again, using the soldering gun with all the brilliance of a brain surgeon. "We connect here, and here. Move this— No!" He almost slapped Lupec's hand away.

The scientist glared daggers at the gawky, almost clownish figure towering over him. But Fellawi shook his head fiercely. "You know about the fission and the critical mass," he said. "But me—I know about bombs."

A few more minutes' work, and Fellawi

119

stepped back. "Ready," he said. "We set the timer now."

Joe couldn't believe his ears. "Set the timer? How are you going to carry that thing when it's armed?"

"Oh, we're not going to carry it," Singh told him. "We're leaving it here."

He smiled at the horrified expressions on the young people's faces. "The other bomb, with the final assembly not completed, will head for the United States tonight. After we've landed in your country, this bomb will go off. When Halifax disappears in a mushroom cloud, your government will have to believe that we can— and *will*—destroy one of your cities. They'll have to set Adyab free."

Singh and Lupec watched as Fellawi set the timer, then started it. "Eight hours," the bomb maker said. "More than enough time."

He put the timer inside, then closed the top of the coffin. His hands were covered now with black graphite lubricant, and one of his knuckles was skinned and bleeding. "We go now?" he asked.

"I am afraid we'll have to leave you," Singh said to the prisoners. "This is why, of course, we were so willing to tell you so much. In an operation like this, we don't need to tie up loose ends." He smiled. "We've already tethered you."

Frank, Joe, and Shauna stood frozen. In less than eight hours the bomb would go off—and they would be vaporized.

"I'll mention your names to Adyab," Singh promised Joe and Frank. "He'll be so happy to hear that you helped gain his freedom."

Chapter

15

FELLAWI SMILED AT Frank. "Goodbye, smart boy." He wasn't making fun of Frank—he meant his compliment sincerely. "I wish I could show you this bomb. *Three* loops inside." He held up three fingers. "But now we go to the place with the funny name. Stony Strand?" He shook his head and went upstairs.

Singh smiled at the retreating genius's back. "For all his brilliance, he never connects the victim with his bombs."

"I think you are the first victims he actually talked to," Lupec added. He gave the prisoners a short, ironic bow. "Gentlemen, lady, our transportation to the States is waiting for us. Goodbye."

Singh just nodded his farewell and barked an order to the guards. Joe thought he had never seen people so happy to be getting out of a room.

At the top of the stairs, Singh paused. "I'll leave the light on, so you can see each other," he said. "We don't want to be cruel, after all."

"Of course not," Joe said sarcastically. "He just wants to light up our lives with this thing." He lunged like a crazy man, trying to kick out at the coffin-bomb. His cuffs and the weight of the coffin he was attached to kept him well short of his target.

"I don't want you to think I'm ungrateful, guys," Shauna MacLaren said. "But I'm starting to wish I'd stayed with the gang from the Hungry Guardsman. At least then I wouldn't know what was going to happen."

She shut her eyes and turned her face away from the coffin.

Joe stopped looking at the bomb, too. He was half-turned away from it, trying to get his left pocket in range of his bound hands. Singh hadn't searched his prisoners—and maybe, just maybe, he'd wind up paying for that oversight.

Twisting himself very uncomfortably, Joe finally managed to jam a couple of fingers into his pocket. He fumbled around until he found the short three-sided file.

He'd popped in a couple of tools when

they'd gone back to the hotel. There was no way—or time—to file through the chains on the handcuffs. But the handle on the file was thin enough to be used as a lockpick. Now, if only he could get it out . . .

His fingers groped for the end of the file. They touched it, lost it, grabbed it again, only to have it slip away. He rubbed his fingertips against his pants. They were getting slick with sweat. He tried again. Got it! Delicately, he pulled the file from his pocket, trying to position his other hand so he could get a better grip on it.

Up above, the cellar door suddenly slammed open. Joe jumped and lost his precarious hold on the file. It tinkled as it hit the floor, but the noise was lost as Fellawi skipped down the stairs.

"I forgot to turn off the soldering iron," he said, shaking his head. "Very bad habit. Dangerous."

He unplugged the tool, brought it back into the private office, then started up the stairs again.

"I don't believe this guy," Frank said. "He sets things up to fry us with an atom bomb, then worries about the dangers of electrical fires. Unbelievable!"

"It probably makes sense from his point of

view," Shauna said. "A fire might set the bomb off prematurely."

"Before he's reached Stony Strand, you mean," Joe said. "What kind of name is that, anyway?"

"It's a small town near the southwest tip of Nova Scotia," Shauna told him. "A fishing village, really. Some of my friends at school come from there. It's very pretty."

"Well, I think it's drawing the wrong kind of tourists," Joe groused.

Frank glanced over at him, his hands busy behind his back. "Did Singh give you any slack on your cuffs? Can you get a hand free?" He struggled a moment more, then shook his head. "Mine are on too tight."

"Mine, too," Joe said.

"How about you, Shauna?" Maybe Singh had taken it easy on the girl.

But she shook her head. "If they were any tighter, they'd be cutting my hands off."

"We've got to figure some way out of this," Frank insisted.

"I almost had one," Joe said, "but it slipped through my fingers." He explained what had happened.

Joe threw himself again at his bonds. "If I get my hands on that Fellawi . . ."

"That's a pretty big if right now," Shauna said. But seeing that the Hardys hadn't given up trying to escape shook her out of her own misery.

"Are there any other tools in your pocket you could use as a pick?" she asked.

Joe shook his head. "That was the only thing thin enough to reach inside."

"Where did it fall?"

"It came down behind me somewhere." Joe scraped around with his running shoe. Then he heard a tiny grating sound beneath his heel. "Here it is."

Carefully scuffing his foot forward, he brought the file into sight.

"It sure looks skinny," Shauna said.

"Let's not mention how useless it is sitting down there." Joe tried a couple of contortions, seeing how close he could get a hand to the floor. But he couldn't even get within two feet of the floor.

"There's no way to reach the stupid thing." Joe brought his foot back, ready to kick the file across the floor. But Shauna stopped him, stretching out her foot to tap his ankle.

Joe looked down at her foot, beginning to get an idea. He waited until he heard the front door slam and a car pull away—final proof that the Assassins were really gone.

"Look," he said to Shauna. "I've got an idea that's pretty far-out, but it might just work to get us out of here."

An hour and a half later they were still working on it. Joe and Shauna had kicked off their shoes and scraped off their socks. Now, with their bare feet, they were trying to pick up the file and get it into Joe's hands.

It was like a stupid summer game they'd play to pass the time at the beach. Shauna would wrap her long toes around the file, and try to lift up her leg. The file would slip away and fall to the floor. They'd both scrabble desperately to make sure it didn't bounce out of reach. They they'd start all over again.

Finally, miraculously, Shauna had caught the file between her toes. She stuck her leg out almost straight from her hip, stretching as far toward Joe as she could.

"That's pretty incredible," Joe said. "How can you do that?"

"Twelve years of ballet classes." Shauna's voice showed a little tremor of strain. "How about doing your part now?"

Joe bent over, straining against his cuffs, aiming with his mouth for the file that wavered so temptingly in front of him.

He had it! The rough part of the file grated against his teeth, but he had a definite hold on it. He straightened up, the file sticking out of his mouth like a long, thin cigar.

"So far, so good," Shauna said. "But how do you get it down to your hands?"

Joe turned back, leaning his head as far over his shoulder as he could. Back, back . . . he pressed against the side of the coffin. Then he opened his lips and let the file fall inside.

Shauna gasped. "All that, and you let it get away from you! We've had it!"

"It didn't get away from me." Joe continued to twist around, looking over his shoulder. "I pulled the little pillow over here to catch the file. And now—" He grunted, straining against the cuffs. "If I can just— Got it!"

Picking the cuff wasn't easy. But it was a lot easier than getting the improvised lockpick into position.

At last, all three of them were out of the cuffs, massaging their wrists.

"Well, let's call the police," Shauna said. "We've got more than enough proof for them now." She stared at the closed coffin-bomb as if she could hear it ticking away.

"That may be too dangerous," Frank said. "This is an Omar Fellawi bomb. His crazy ways of putting them together have blown up a lot of bomb-disposal types. It may take better experts than can be found in Halifax. And I don't think there's enough time left to fly anyone in."

"So what are you saying?" Shauna cried.

"He's saying that he's probably the only person in town who's beaten an Omar Fellawi bomb." Joe stared hard at his brother. "Do you think you can do it?"

Frank took a deep breath. "I don't think we've got much choice."

He approached the coffin, remembering how Fellawi had touched it first. Running his fingers along to find the tightening bolt, he found a small button and pushed it. Then, behind the handle, another button. And there was another one, down at the foot of the casket.

Frank picked up the cover. Nothing happened. He gasped when he saw the timer. More time had passed than he thought. "Okay," he said, "we know where the final assembly went in. If we get that out, and cut the detonator for the charge that's supposed to blow it into the other chunk of uranium, we should be home free."

He pulled out the circuit tracer from his pocket. "Joe, see if you can find me some wire clippers. And bring back that soldering gun."

Frank spent an hour of agony crouched over the big bomb, tracking circuits, disconnecting wires, slowly undoing what Fellawi had built. He'd found the cylinder of the final assembly. Fellawi had surrounded it with a maze of circuitry, including two of those infamous loops.

He found trap after trap and cut those circuits out. Sweat ran down his face, burning his eyes. He had to be absolutely perfect. It wasn't just his life on the line, or Joe's, or Shauna's. Frank was carrying an entire city on his shoulders.

At last he was ready to slide out the final assembly. He eased the cylinder out of its sleeve, the graphite lubricant making his fingers black and slippery.

Then he stopped. What was that over there, against the blackness? Frank traced along the outside of the cylinder with his finger. He could hardly see it, but he could feel it. Fellawi had set a booby trap like the wires looped around the plastique in his bomb in the Citadel. But this time he'd used a black wire against the black graphite.

Holding the assembly exactly where it was, he turned to Joe and said, "Get me some wire from the desk, please. And get your knife out for me."

With a nice big piece of wire and Joe's pocketknife, Frank was able to construct a loop of his own—a bypass loop. Now he had lots of room to slip the deadly cylinder out.

"Okay. One down, one to go." He let out a deep sigh. Whatever happened now, the city was safe.

It took another forty minutes to disarm the detonator. By the time he was done, Frank's hands were black, bruised, and scratched from fumbling around the insides of the bomb. But

Omar Fellawi's deadly creation was now just a lot of junk machinery in a fancy coffin.

"Now it's time to call the cops," Frank said.

Maybe he was too tired from tackling the bomb. He should have foreseen the police reaction.

They'd gotten Detective Otley out of bed. He wore a suit and tie, but Joe had the suspicion that his shirt was actually a pajama top. Sitting in the office of the funeral parlor, he listened as the kids explained the connection to the attack on Dundee.

"So this is the fort he was talking about, huh?" He sleepily nodded his head.

His eyes opened a lot wider when they mentioned what was in the coffin in the storeroom. "An atomic bomb? And you disarmed it?" His tone was frankly disbelieving. "Well, if it won't go off, we may as well leave it for later this morning. I'm leaving a guard at this site, going home to sleep, and expect to see you this morning—at a more decent hour."

"But the Assassins will get away with the other bomb!" Joe burst out.

"Kid, I'm having a very hard time believing any of this," Otley told him. "And you're not helping things by yelling. I'll see you in the morning. *Period.*"

"You might at least call the RCMP," Frank suggested.

"And wake them up at this ungodly hour with a story like this? Later for you, pal—much later."

Joe, Frank, and Shauna stepped out of the house into the predawn darkness.

"They'll be long gone by the time you get to see Otley," Shauna predicted gloomily.

"That means it's up to us to stop that bomb from leaving for the States." Joe turned to Shauna. "Do you know the way to Stony Strand?"

Chapter

16

"SHOW YOU HOW to get to Stony Strand?" Shauna said. "I'll do better than that. We have to find a phone."

They got a lift back to their hotel from the police. While Frank and Joe got some soda from the machine in the hallway, Shauna went to work on the phone.

"All set," she said, smiling mysteriously when they returned to the room. "We have to be downstairs in half an hour to catch our ride."

"So, tell us more about this Stony Strand place," Joe said.

"It's about thirty miles from here, on the south coast," Shauna said. "About twenty thousand years ago, the last Ice Age scraped away all the topsoil from the area. Settlers called the place Stony Strand because the beaches are ledges of solid rock.''

"Solid rock?'' Frank said.

"*Solid,*'' Shauna repeated. "The first time I went down there, someone pointed out a graveyard. It was the last place in about twenty miles where the soil was deep enough for burying people.''

Joe gave her a look. "That's a nice, pleasant thought to start off this little jaunt.''

Half an hour later they stood outside the hotel in the predawn chill. They'd dressed as warmly as they could, and Shauna looked a little like a refugee in Joe's jacket.

The ride Shauna had promised turned out to be two rides—a car and a van. The guy who leaned out from the driver's seat of the car looked vaguely familiar.

"Frank and Joe Hardy, meet my friend Charlie Bell,'' Shauna said, taking care of the introductions. "He's a corporal up at the Citadel.''

"*That's* where we saw you before,'' Joe said.

"I'm harder to recognize out of uniform,'' Charlie said with a grin. "But there are some good things about being a corporal.''

He led the way to the van and opened the back door. Five guys sat in the back, besides the driver. "This is my squad," Charlie said. "Will's behind the wheel, and these are Robert, Ken, Doug, Jack, and Harry. Guys, meet Frank and Joe Hardy."

His corporal's guard was out of uniform. But Frank noted that each of the guys in the back of the van clutched the antique rifle he'd been using up at the Citadel.

"When Charlie called and told us what you'd done for us," one of the guys—Ken—said, "we thought you could use some reinforcements."

He grinned as he patted his big rifle. "It's a hundred and forty years old, but this is all the firepower we could get our hands on."

"Let's hope we don't need to use it," Frank said.

"Well, let's get this show on the road," Charlie said. "You guys will be riding with me. I'll be guiding Will."

"Remember how I said I had friends from Stony Strand?" Shauna said. "Well, Charlie's one of them."

Frank nodded. "I'm glad we have someone who knows the area."

They set off west from the downtown area, skirting an arm of the harbor, then heading inland for a while. The road looped its way to the south, then curved west again as it approached the south shore.

Charlie drove steadily through the murky dawn. Joe could hardly make out the landmarks Shauna pointed to. Frank was asleep in the back seat beside him.

Rolling to a stop at the crest of a hill, Charlie said, "We're here."

Frank roused himself to look down on a scene that should have been on a postcard. Stony Strand was little more than a village, a handful of gaily painted and weather-beaten houses scattered along the shore of a small cove. Piers lined an inlet from the cove, where fishing boats bobbed at anchor.

The sun still wasn't all the way up, but fingers of telltale gray were appearing in the east. Stony Strand's fishermen had been up and about for at least an hour. Charlie was invaluable. As a local boy, he was able to ask if any strangers were staying in the area.

One grizzled old salt nodded. "Someone's renting the old Garth place—you know, the cottage on the headland."

Charlie knew it all too well. "When we were kids, that was the town's haunted house. Somebody fixed it up to rent to summer tourists." He frowned. "They couldn't have chosen a better spot for themselves."

"Why?" Joe asked.

"You'll see."

They drove as close as they dared, hiding the vehicles behind a house that belonged to friends of Charlie's family. Then they marched on through the murky early morning light to the foot of the headland.

Wet fog blew in from the bay as they made their way across rocky terrain that looked as if it would be more at home on the moon. They had to place their feet carefully—the fog had made the naked rock slick underfoot.

Finally they reached the headland. A light breeze tore a hole in the curtain of fog, and Joe understood what Charlie had been talking about.

The cottage perched on a slight rise at the tip of the headland. To get to it, they'd have to move across a hundred feet of naked, broken granite. The neck of land was only fifteen or twenty feet wide in places. One man with a pistol could hold off a small army.

"This fog is a lucky break," Charlie said, kneeling behind a clump of boulders and peering out at the house. "They won't be able to leave until it begins to clear."

"You live around here. Can we use it to get closer to the house?" Frank asked. "Or will it lift too soon?"

"We'll have to try," Charlie said with a shrug. He started setting up his tiny force.

"Robert, Jack, and Doug, you're our best marksmen. Stay here behind these rocks and lay down cover fire if we need it. The rest of you will move up with me and the Hardys."

He glanced at Shauna, but she just smiled and shook her head. "I've had enough playing with guns tonight."

"Okay," Charlie said. "Load your firelocks."

His men grounded their guns, pulled out little paper cartridges, poured the powder down the muzzles, then pushed a bullet down with a ramrod. Placing a percussion cap under the hammer of the gun, they were ready.

"Takes a while to load those guys, doesn't it?" Joe said.

"It's worse than you think," Charlie said as he shoved a bullet home in his own gun. "To use this ramrod right, you almost *have* to stand up."

Joe looked at the uneven, rocky surface they'd have to move across. Anyone standing to reload would be a sitting duck. "You guys better hold your fire until we know it will do some good."

Rifles at the ready, Charlie and his troops set off down the headland in a ragged skirmish line. To the rear, the covering force hunkered down behind the boulders. Frank and Joe, crouching low, crept ahead of Charlie's force.

They made it almost three-quarters of the way to the house before they bumped into a guard.

The guy was sitting against a rock, half-asleep, when Frank came upon him. Caught by surprise, the man half rose, trying to bring up his Uzi.

Frank snapped out a kick that knocked the guy back against the rock, out cold. His gun clattered to the ground.

That was enough noise to wake up another guard closer to the house. He asked something in a foreign language while Frank groped for the lost weapon.

The man spoke again, a nervous edge to his voice.

Then the worst happened. The fog began to lift.

Charlie and his troops appeared through the thinning grayness like ghosts. The guard yelled and leveled his Uzi. But Joe popped up from behind a rock, his arm already swinging in a roundhouse right. Now they had two down, but that left two guards from the funeral home unaccounted for.

They soon put in an appearance, firing wildly with their machine guns. Charlie and company ducked to the ground, finding whatever cover they could among the rugged rocks. The three guys left in the boulders opened fire, driving the guards back indoors.

It was a weird sort of battle—the latest in automatic firepower against weapons that were antiques a century ago. The Assassins could spit three bullets a second at their enemies. Charlie's guys were lucky to manage two shots in a minute.

One of the Assassins took advantage of the long reload time to lean out the window and spray bullets around the rock where Charlie lay. Frank answered with half a clip from his Uzi, driving the guy back inside.

A moment later the other guard tried a charge, throwing open the door. The heavy bullet from one of Charlie's guys hit the door, sending the man staggering back.

The firing died down as a sort of stalemate developed. The Assassins couldn't come out of the house, but the Hardys and their friends couldn't get in.

"Is Frank Hardy there?" Singh's voice rang out in the sudden silence.

"Yes," Frank shouted back.

"So, you disabled our bomb. And all this shooting will surely bring the authorities. A pity." The rock Frank hid behind was spattered with machine-gun fire.

In fact, bullets were flying all along the headland from the windows of the house. It was as though the people inside weren't worried about saving ammunition.

Then Frank saw why, as the last of the fog cleared away. The guards were wasting bullets as a delaying action. They had to keep the attackers' heads down so the brains of the operation could escape.

And escape they would if the Hardys didn't do something about it. Beyond the house stretched a small pier.

And at the end of the pier was a seaplane, and the plane's props were already beginning to spin.

Chapter

17

FRANK HARDY POPPED up, fired a quick burst from his Uzi, then ducked behind the rock again as the Assassins sent a hail of bullets his way.

He had slid behind a different rock, working his way back to Charlie and the guys from the Citadel. The problem was, the next stretch of rock behind him was bare and flat. There was no cover at all. How could he get across?

Joe must have seen the problem, because now he popped up to fire a couple of shots. That drew the enemy's fire his way as Frank dashed across the open space.

Covering each other, the Hardys finally managed to reach Charlie's position.

"Take this," Joe said, handing over his Uzi. "It will help even up the sides a little." He pointed at the pier, where even now three figures had appeared. "Use it to pin them down, to keep them from reaching the plane."

"What are you going to do?" Charlie asked.

"I'm going for a swim," Joe replied. "With luck, I may be able to convince that pilot to delay his departure."

"I'm doing the same," Frank said, passing his gun to another of the student soldiers. "Do the best you can till we get out there."

"You're going swimming—here?" Charlie said. "The undertow can kill you."

"The undertow isn't the only thing," Joe said with a grin. "You worry about keeping those guys from crossing the pier. We'll worry about getting to the plane."

"Of course, if they start shooting at us, we wouldn't mind a little covering fire," Frank added.

Charlie nodded, rising for a second to deliver a quick burst from his Uzi. The three figures on the pier scattered and hit the deck.

"You'd better get going," Charlie said. "The bullets in this clip won't last forever."

The Hardys made their way to a rocky ledge

by the water, concealed by a big upthrust boulder. They took off their shoes and socks, then Joe stuck a foot into the water. "Cold," he announced. "And that undertow is— Whoa!" The force of the current sucked him right off the slippery rocks.

Frank slid in after him, bracing himself for the sudden cold. The undertow pulled hungrily at him, trying to take him out to sea. But that's where Frank wanted to go. He didn't have to fight to get back to land. As long as he headed for the seaplane, he'd be all right.

Of course, if the seaplane took off before he reached it, it would be a long swim to Maine.

Frank tried not to think about that. He just concentrated on the seaplane. Both he and Joe spent most of their time swimming underwater, rising only to catch a breath of air and to make sure they were heading the right way.

Once when he broke the surface, Frank heard gunfire. He glanced over at the pier. The three figures were making it closer to the plane. Could he beat them?

He struck out a little stronger as he swam.

Now he began to feel all the exhaustion he'd held back while he worked over the bomb. Fighting the undertow was a little trickier than he'd expected, too. It pulled at him like a hungry beast that wanted to be fed.

Frank sucked air and kept struggling. Then

. . . what was this in front of him? The pontoon for the seaplane!

He reached up to grab on—and his hand slipped off. The undertow tore at him now, as if it were afraid he might escape. He was going down. . . .

A strong hand grabbed onto his collar, hauling him back up to the air. Joe Hardy grinned down at him, one hand on a strut of the plane, one still twisted in his shirt.

"Hey, big brother," he whispered. "You don't want to miss the party now."

They crept along the pontoon, concealed from the Assassins by the fuselage of the plane. It was very slippery going—one wrong move would leave them at the mercy of the undertow. Finally Joe reached the passenger door.

He pulled it open and swung in on the astonished pilot. By the time Frank got in, the pilot lay in the back of the plane, deep in dreamland.

Frank settled himself in the pilot's seat. "Okay," he said. "Let's see if those ground-training classes were worth the money Dad paid."

He checked the instruments, trying to find the engine controls. Outside on the pier, the shooting suddenly reached the proportions of a small war. The nasty rattle of submachine guns had a desperate sound.

The group on the pier had almost reached the plane now. Frank recognized them at once. Lupec, pale and staring, scuttled along. Tall, gangling Fellawi moved carefully, his hands cradling a lead box like the one he'd carried the night before.

Frank realized that must be the final assembly for the second bomb. He glanced in the back of the plane and saw a big crate. So, the rest was already on board.

Singh was the last of the three. He kept facing the headland, a MAC-10 in his hands, spraying bullets to keep the Citadel kids down. The whiteness of his gritted teeth showed against the dark of his mustache.

There was no more time to study the situation. Frank reached out, flicking switches, adjusting controls. The engines, which had only been idling, roared into life. The propellers began to turn in earnest now. Leaping against its moorings, the seaplane was ready to fly.

Frank let out the throttle on one engine, while pulling back on the other. He jockeyed the stick. Slowly, the seaplane began to swing around.

Singh caught the movement and turned around, his eyes becoming round when he recognized Frank and Joe in the cockpit.

He didn't have a chance to do anything else. The seaplane's wing swept over the pier, scraping Singh, Fellawi, and Lupec straight into the water.

"You're lucky those three didn't drown," Detective Otley told the Hardys a little later. The headland was now crawling with police, Halifax cops, provincial police, even some RCMP—although Joe was disappointed to see they weren't wearing their snappy red uniforms.

"None of these guys would have been any great loss to humanity," Joe said. "Besides, we caught them all before they went out to sea."

They'd dragged the three chief terrorists out of the water like drowned rats. Singh had lost his gun, but Fellawi was the most upset. The final assembly for his bomb had slipped from his fingers. Who knew where the undertow would take it?

"We'll have divers looking for that piece of the bomb," Otley said, almost reading Joe's mind. "But what about these guys? The head Mountie told me that Assassins take poison rather than be captured."

"Well, Lupec and Fellawi weren't really Assassins," Joe explained. "They were only working on contract. As for Singh—I guess he was in too much shock to do the job. We had his poison pellet out of his hollow tooth before we gave him mouth-to-mouth."

"I had some professors from Dalhousie University looking that bomb over early this morning," Otley said. "They nearly had fits when they realized what it was." He glanced over at Frank. "They also told me that we have a lot to thank you for."

Frank waved that off. "Just make sure my name doesn't get into the papers—that is, if the papers ever get to write anything about this."

"You don't think they will?" Joe said.

"Governments get a little nervous about announcing things like this," Frank said. "This whole story could just become another nuclear secret."

"That's fine with me," Shauna MacLaren said. "I'd prefer to forget about the whole thing. Halifax doesn't need to know it just escaped an atomic explosion." She managed a smile. "Besides, my thing is building stuff, not blowing it up."

She winked at Joe, who smiled back. "You'll have to come back and have another free dinner," she said to him. "We can't have you going around saying that the Hungry Guardsman blows up at the least little thing."

Joe laughed. "I'd like that," he said.

She got a little more serious as she looked

up at him. "I would, too. Well, maybe you'll have more depositions to collect—"

"Oh, no!" Frank said. "We haven't even gotten the ones we were sent here for!"

"Don't worry," said Otley. "They're on Gerry Dundee's desk. You can have them by this afternoon."

"How is Sergeant Dundee?" Frank asked. "We checked in on him yesterday, but since then . . ."

"I know," Otley said. "Things got a little hectic. Well, the good news is that he's going to pull through."

"That's great," said Joe.

Otley went on. "The bad news is that he's through as a cop. He suppressed your report, went off on his own, and nearly got himself killed. Like it or not, he's going to retire."

"Sounds tough on him," Shauna said.

Otley nodded. "You said it. This guy is all cop."

"Still, he'll go out in a blaze of glory. He smashed a terrorist ring," Joe said.

"Maybe more than we know." Frank thought of Sandy White in a prison somewhere. He wasn't going to get out. The questioning would continue. Maybe the questioners would get the information they needed to smash the terrorists once and for all.

"And, of course, he helped save Halifax," Joe went on. "That's nothing to sneeze at."

Frank nodded. "There are worse ways to go," he said. "Much worse ways."

Frank and Joe's next case:

During a daring robbery of rare gems, the Hardys spot the thief. Their old enemy Charity has turned up in Bayport—and once again she manages to slip through their fingers. Frank and Joe track her to San Diego, where they run smack into a crooks' convention.

A group of master criminals is planning the crime of the century—and they think Joe is one of the dishonored guests. Joe joins the gang, but then he disappears in a bomb blast. Frank is left to avenge his brother's death against all odds as he tackles a killer tag team with a secret weapon—and a lethal lady named Charity . . . in *Thick as Thieves*, Case #29 in The Hardy Boys Casefiles™.